1-800-SUMMER

JOSIE RIVIERA

This book is dedicated to all my wonderful readers who have supported me every inch of the way.
THANK YOU!

CHAPTER 1

The stable carried the scents of hay and leather, and Belle Boots took in the weathered wooden planks, the plastic buckets of water, the wide mirror propped in the corner of the stall.

And, most notably, at Jenkins, her sweet, colorful appaloosa, all one thousand pounds of quirky loyalty and claustrophobia.

"We're leaving, handsome." She fished in her pocket for a carrot. "Off we trot to greener pastures."

Jenkins whinnied and poked his nose through the stall, noisily accepting the carrot and ignoring her quip.

"Why is the pasture greener?" She rubbed his ears. "Because the new landlord of my sorry excuse for an apartment raised the rent." Which meant fewer than five weeks to find another place. She grabbed a water bucket and brush, scrubbing and refilling the bucket. "Maybe this is the ideal opportunity for us to return to Wilmington."

Another crunch of the carrot, and Jenkins pawed the stable floor.

"I can't play right now. I'm sorry. My therapy sessions begin in an hour."

In the past two years, she'd grown fond of the postcard-perfect community of Roses. In fact, she regarded Roses as her hometown.

She let a breath go slowly. Or did she?

Sometimes a person needed to leave a place to discover where home truly was. The sense of adventure that had surged through her when she had decided on Roses—the thrill of a different town and untried places—had worn thin. Despite her efforts to stay busy, Belle had never gotten over her loneliness since she had left Wilmington.

Perhaps she was simply homesick. She missed Aunt Lucinda, her mother's older sister and Belle's only living relative. Plus, she missed the ocean—the bracing waves, the salty air rushing across her face, and the sunbeams flashing off the water like silent jewels.

Jenkins stamped his hoof, bringing Belle back to the present.

"I only brought one carrot with me," she said. "I'll return later this afternoon with more."

In the pale-yellow light filtering through the slats, the echoes of a late May morning drifted, and promised a typical North Carolina day. Sunrises were cool and bearable before the humidity and oppressive heat kicked in.

After she mucked the stall and turned out Jenkins to the pasture, Belle's attentions swung back to her dilemma. Wilmington beckoned. Or perhaps Florida or California.

Only one thing was certain. She was moving. The destination could wait.

She glanced at her watch. Swiftly, she washed and sprinted to her pickup truck. In the tangle of the confusing morning, she'd lost track of time.

Her first equine therapy session was with Joseph, a

dark-eyed boy whose lean legs raced so quickly he reminded her of a clockwork figure. His adoptive parents, Candee and Teddy, owned a large Victorian home on Thompson Lane and had built a riding ring on their acreage.

The second session was with Megan Bransfield, a chubby, pale girl who wore a bright pink patch over her right eye and rarely smiled.

How could she desert these precious children? Belle's sentiments wrestled between anguish and indecision. At the other side of the spectrum, anticipation welled.

THE DRIVE into Roses went slower than expected, which invariably happened whenever she was in a hurry. When she neared the Thompson Lane turn-off, she took in the scene in front of her—red, white, and blue balloons; the local marching band; and a banner stretching across the main street announcing the Memorial Day parade.

Quietly groaning, she clicked on her right signal, pulled to the curb, and phoned Candee.

"Hi, Belle," came Candee's cheerful response.

"Candee, I apologize." Belle rolled down her window, and a welcoming breeze gusted in, tousling her ponytail. "I'm running late, and traffic is at a standstill."

"No worries," Candee replied. "We'll wait for you."

"If you and your family prefer to attend the parade, it's fine. We can reschedule."

"Joseph wouldn't miss his session with you for anything in the world. Teddy and I appreciate all you've done, because Joseph's transformation is remarkable. He's considerably more outgoing and upbeat."

Belle's compassion squeezed. *Tell Candee gently.*

Belle and Candee had engaged in numerous coffee chats,

most of which had centered around Belle's ex-husband, Tyler.

She'd married him at twenty-three years old. He was stoic and impassive and a suitable complement to Belle's over-the-top eagerness to please. And, they had hoped for a large family.

Or so she'd thought.

She yanked her mind back to Candee's enthusiastic, one-sided dialogue regarding her barbecue that evening.

"I have news," Belle blurted.

"What?"

"This session will be Joseph's last, at least with me." Belle fiddled with her truck's side-view mirror as an emptiness hollowed out a pit in her stomach. It wasn't in her nature to abandon her clientele, most notably the children who relied on her.

"Why is this his last session?" Candee asked.

"I'm moving." *So much for gently.* "Soon."

"So sudden?"

"My rent was raised to an astronomical amount. The new landlord said his parents are relocating to a retirement community, and he is taking over the property."

"Astronomical?"

"He didn't exactly use the word astronomical, but he offered a marathon explanation and got his point across."

"Can't you find somewhere else close by to live? Teddy and I have extra bedrooms on the third floor. What's more, Desiree and Kieran are hardly ever home. I'm certain they wouldn't mind if you lived with them for a while, either."

Desiree was Candee's sister, and she and her husband lived a few houses away from Candee. Kieran had opened O'Malley's, an Irish restaurant which had become tremendously well-liked. Desiree had set her profession as a lawyer on hold in order to assist Kieran.

"I refuse to inconvenience anyone," Belle replied.

"You're no inconvenience, and your horse can stable here."

"Jenkins? One never can predict how he'll behave."

"We're currently only boarding Joseph's and Megan's horses. Besides, Jenkins is a sweetie—despite his behavioral issues."

Belle chuckled. "He'll figure out a way to get out of his stall and invite the other horses to slip away with him."

"He did that once, right? When he was a racehorse?"

"He was tired of being a racehorse and has adapted to becoming a riding horse." Although Jenkins was notorious for bucking off a forceful advanced rider by stopping fast ensuring the unsuspecting rider sailed over him.

"At present, Jenkins is happy," Candee said.

"As long as everything goes his way. Though I'm thinking practically, and any arrangements in Roses would be merely temporary." Belle added a smile to her words to soften her refusal. "Thank you for your offer, though."

"Roses is home."

"For you." Belle shifted her attention back to the road. "Not for me. My home is in Wilmington, where my roots are."

Wilmington? Roots? She'd made a decision?

Apparently yes, at least in her subconscious.

"Teddy has contacts in Wilmington," Candee was saying. "Besides, I'm a Realtor. Are you looking for anyplace special?

"I'd like to live near the ocean. We'll talk more when I arrive."

The women said their goodbyes and hung up.

As Belle merged into traffic, the slam of a door broke her concentration. A man strode onto a second-floor balcony and leaned over the railing. His broad shoulders were starkly outlined in a crisp white shirt. His breaths were slow and deliberate.

And then he did something completely out of character—considering the elegant house, his tailored silhouette, and the passing motorists who could witness his despair.

He placed his head in his hands.

Belle craned her neck. Was he weeping? Should she offer support?

Behind her, a car horn beeped, and she twisted back to the policewoman directing traffic. Caught in the uneasy silence of indecision, Belle followed the policewoman's signals and kept moving.

One last time, she turned. Just as the cars picked up speed, the man raised his head. For an instant, their gazes met.

He was incredibly handsome, in a Kevin Costner sort of way. His hair was dark with a hint of crimson, layered and expertly cut. His lips were firmly drawn.

And Belle couldn't help noticing that his cheeks were wet with tears. Swiftly, he mopped his eyes with a handkerchief, and the vulnerable gesture touched her heart.

AN HOUR LATER, she pulled her truck into the driveway of Candee's Victorian style home.

On the lush, expansive front yard, Joseph swung on a rope swing tied to the limb of an enormous oak tree. His thin legs kicked vigorously and the tree branch bent in an arc as Candee pushed him back and forth.

As soon as he spotted Belle, Joseph jumped off the swing and scurried to her. "Miss Belle!" He reached up and quickly hugged her. "Did you get to see the parade?"

"You are more important than a parade." Belle pressed back tears, reminding herself there were other excellent horse therapists in the area.

She slung her backpack over her shoulder. Joseph's brown eyes sparkled with mischief, his complexion glowed healthy and tanned. After his father had died in a horrific car accident, Candee and Teddy had steered him through several difficult years. Teddy was Joseph's uncle, and he and Candee had legally adopted the little boy.

Belle scrubbed a hand over his dark wavy hair. "Let's get started, shall we?"

An irresistible giggle lit his expression. With an "okay," he tore down the driveway as Candee fell in step beside Belle.

"Teddy is in the stable and will help Joseph saddle up the horse," Candee said. "I informed him about your move."

Because of his home-flipping and construction dealings, Teddy teamed up with workers across the state. Along with Rob, his partner—who also resided in Roses with his wife, Kathleen—their supportive network of crewmen was substantial.

"What did Teddy say?" Belle prompted.

"He provided several leads, and I found a Wilmington rental available at a reasonable price. The landlords are a young couple." Candee tucked a strand of red hair behind her ear. "The apartment is located a few blocks from the beach and is situated on a modest amount of acreage. The couple is giving up farming, but keeping their house and barn and outbuildings. They'll allow you to use their stable and grounds, because they're both taking full-time jobs in Wilmington."

"What is the rental amount?" Belle asked.

"Three hundred dollars a month."

"Perfect. The situation sounds ideal."

"*Almost* ideal," Candee hedged. "The property needs work, judging from the description and photos."

"Do you have any information?" Belle asked.

"All on my phone. Let's review everything tonight when

you come to my barbecue. Rob and Kathleen are coming, and Rob is baking a batch of his marvelous muffins. Kieran and Desiree are bringing Irish pub food from their restaurant." Candee laughed. "A traditional, all-American buffet with a dash of Irish flavor and delectable desserts."

Belle pushed out a sigh. "I'd love to attend, but I can't. I need to start packing."

Candee pulled out her cellphone. "Then I'll text you the information."

There was a recognizable whoosh followed by a ping as photos appeared on Belle's phone. She scrolled through, scrutinizing each one.

"I like the apartment," she murmured.

Candee peered over Belle's shoulder. "It has charm and character."

"Is that your Realtor's way of describing the paint that's peeling off the ceiling?" Belle enlarged the kitchen photo. "I'll help clean."

"You won't need to, because Teddy will provide a crew and charge a nominal fee for repairs." Candee placed a hand on Belle's arm. "I know you're going to object, but please don't because we insist."

The first shred of optimism broke through Belle's concerns. Candee was a true friend, and her relocation might go easier than she anticipated. She extended a heartfelt thank you.

"Are you done talking to my Mom?" Joseph called out while Teddy led Blackjack, Joseph's sleek black horse, from the stable.

"Yes. I'm coming." Belle placed her backpack near the fence and hastened toward them. Later, she'd ask Candee for another referral, just in case this rental didn't work out. Then again, perhaps the apartment was fate.

But fate was a funny thing.

. . .

AFTER JOSEPH'S SESSION ENDED, Megan appeared at the riding ring, the familiar pink patch covering her right eye. Her crimson-colored hair fell to her shoulders in slight curls, a startling contrast to her fair complexion and freckled features.

"Hi, Megan!" Belle greeted.

While Candee, Joseph and Teddy tended to Blackjack, Belle saddled Megan's pony, Honeycrisp, and led the solid Haflinger out of the stable, securing the pony to the fence with a halter rope.

A nanny normally brought Megan to her sessions, but today a man brought her.

A man with dark hair, enhanced by a hint of crimson.

An incredibly handsome man.

An incredibly familiar man.

He strode to the fence with Megan clinging tightly to his hand. As always, her riding boots were sturdy, her jeans washed and pressed.

"Hi, Miss Belle," the child said.

"Megan, you look so pretty." Belle bent to greet her. "If it's Monday morning, then it's time for your session with Honeycrisp."

Megan nodded.

As Belle straightened, the man eyed Belle, and then Honeycrisp. He wiped a hand along his pinstriped suit coat and stepped backward.

"I'm Andrew Bransfield," he said. "Are you the instructor?"

"Daddy." Megan giggled, her dimpled cheeks expanding in a wide grin as she handed Belle her riding bag. "Miss Belle teaches me every week."

His expression held no glimmer of recognition. He

9

merely stared at Belle while her own pulse gave a leap of acknowledgment.

"Hello, Mr. Bransfield," she managed. "It's a pleasure to meet you."

She accepted Megan's bag and dug through it until she found the riding helmet. She crouched to fasten the helmet under Megan's chin.

"Andrew."

"I'm sorry?" Belle glanced up.

"Please, call me Andrew."

"Andrew," Belle repeated. She stood, tightened her ponytail, and extended a friendly grin. Wow, up close he was even handsomer than she'd thought. And she couldn't determine from his clear, emerald-colored eyes whether he'd actually wept on the balcony. Perhaps she'd imagined the entire scenario.

Or perhaps he'd experienced a moment of desolation he couldn't contain.

Desolation was completely acceptable, wasn't it? She'd suffered through it, especially after her divorce.

She kept her grin. "I'm glad you're here so I can speak with you, Mr. Bransfield."

"Andrew." He returned her grin with one of his own. "Is anything wrong?"

She pressed her lips together, grappling to find the right words. "Megan is making excellent progress."

Coward. Tell him you're leaving and this will be his daughter's last session with you.

"She is, isn't she?" He gazed at Megan. "And she's adorable in her pink riding helmet."

"She certainly is. And we believe in safety first."

Brilliant, Belle. As if a father wouldn't understand the importance of safety for his little girl.

Andrew regarded his daughter with unabashed pride.

"The doctor said that the patch therapy for her lazy eye made a difference. Her eyes are beginning to work together."

"That's such good news," Belle replied.

Still wearing his shiny blue helmet, Joseph ran up to them. "My parents are in the stable," he assured, as he and Megan skipped away hand in hand. Amused and impressed by their easy camaraderie, Belle smiled. While Joseph often giggled during his sessions, Megan's lips usually never spared a curve.

"I'll be along shortly," Belle called after them.

"So, I'm finally meeting the famous Belle." A lyrical Scottish accent enhanced Andrew's baritone voice. She pictured him wearing a kilt, knee socks, and a clan badge, rather than a business suit.

"I can assure that I lead a quiet, uneventful life."

"In these parts, you are remarkable."

"Hardly." Compared to his voice, hers sounded fluttery and breathy.

His presence was commanding, partly because of his six-foot tall frame, and partly because of the self-confidence he exuded. And his smile. Oh, his smile did funny things to her pulse. Gone was the bleak man from the balcony.

In his pinstriped suit and carrying a leather briefcase, he seemed completely out of his element in the dusty surroundings of a riding ring. He belonged in an uptown high-rise office on Wall Street.

Yet, despite his buttoned-up appearance, a lock of that crimson-colored hair fell across his temple, giving him a slightly disheveled appeal.

In any event, he was far too fine looking for his own good. And from her limited experience with men, he was probably well aware of his charisma.

"Here in Roses, your skill is renowned," he said. "Megan's

physician recommended equine therapy. I checked numerous references before I chose you."

"Horses have the best hearts and are excellent listeners."

"I was referring to you, not the horses." He rubbed the back of his neck and eyed Honeycrisp.

"Horses are awesome."

"Sure." His jaw set. That is, until he smiled. "Your skills are highly regarded."

"Thank you." He didn't provide her the opportunity to refute his obvious dislike of horses. "I love these kids. I love my job." Belle ignored Candee's scrutiny as she and Megan emerged from the stable. Teddy, with a wave, strode to the house with Joseph.

"How about a proper hello?"

"We've been talking for several minutes."

"But a proper handshake comes first." He reached out his hand, sending an unexpected quiver through her as their fingers touched.

Oh, my. What on earth?

She kept her hand in his, although she should let go. Shouldn't she?

As she ended their handshake, she focused on the ground.

The ensuing silence between them was interrupted only by chirping birds and chattering squirrels.

"Are you captivated by dirt?" he inquired.

"Candee made certain the ground was ideal for a ring. You see … clay-based soil is the best for riding because …" She was babbling. She never babbled. To her chagrin, her cheeks overheated.

No, no. This was absurd. She wasn't a woman who melted because a man shook her hand.

Candee called out and Belle performed a smooth turn.

"I'm coming," she replied, then turned. "Mr. Bransfield …"

"Andrew."

He backed up, keeping a watchful eye on Honeycrisp.

On several occasions, Megan had confided that her father didn't like horses.

Or was he afraid of them?

With a knowing grin, Belle nodded in Honeycrisp's direction, admiring the horse's flaxen blond mane and tail. "You purchased a stunning horse for your daughter."

"Right."

Belle hurried to Megan as she climbed up on the mounting block. The child put her foot in the stirrup, grabbed the saddle horn, and swung onto the horse.

"I promise there's nothing to fear," Belle called out. "Horses are gentle."

"In your opinion," he returned. "In mine, horses are large and awkward."

"Honeycrisp is small. A pony, actually. She's only thirteen hands."

"That's a lot of hands," came his quick reply.

WHEN MEGAN'S SESSION ENDED, Belle became distinctly aware of the laughing conversation between Mr. Bransfield and Candee as they stood outside the fence.

She extended a professional smile as Candee entered the ring.

"I'll tend to the horses while you and Andrew talk." Candee snatched Honeycrisp's halter rope and, with Megan, led the pony's return to the stable.

"Miss Belle? May I have a word with you?" Mr. Bransfield unlocked the gate and cautiously stepped into the riding ring. "It is *Miss* Belle, isn't it?"

"Yes." She wondered how he'd learned she wasn't married. Most likely, Candee had told him. And, Belle didn't wear a wedding band. Her attention dropped to his ring finger. No wedding band, either. "But may I ask *you* something first?"

He scowled.

Belle glanced over her shoulder to be certain Candee had let the horses out into the adjoining pasture to graze and drink at the creek. When she faced him again, he watched her with quiet contemplation.

"I saw you in town," Belle began. "In any event, I believe it was you."

"Because it *was* me."

He muttered in a Gaelic dialect she didn't understand. Nonetheless, she drew a breath and forged ahead. "Whatever happened that made you so upset on the balcony?"

CHAPTER 2

*a*ndrew kept his expression carefully bland. "What led you to believe that was my house?"

His challenge was an excuse to pause while he fitted his response into a plausible answer. He wouldn't admit he was prone to tears. Nor would he discuss his former wife's behavior regarding her interest in their daughter.

Or rather, her disinterest.

His divorce had induced him to frustration, anger, and heartache. Megan deserved her mother's love. Weren't mothers supposed to be devoted to their children?

"That was you on the balcony, wasn't it?" Belle asked.

"Yes, we've established that."

"We have?"

"We have now."

"You looked ... distressed. I considered stopping my truck to come help you."

"Were you planning on rushing up to rescue me?"

Okay, that snappish reply was uncalled for. He softened his response with a quiet "sorry."

"I like to help." She sighed. "Were you rattled about a business deal that went wrong?"

"Rattled?" *Another question, another deflection, another ploy to delay responding.*

"Distressed … troubled …." She glanced sideways. "I was concerned."

"No need. I can take care of myself." He sent an indifferent shrug.

Nonetheless, she was obviously worried and there was no disdain in her voice. Again, his reaction had been uncalled for. "Are you normally this inquisitive, Miss Belle?"

"No." A hint of embarrassment crept into her gentle voice, along with a pink blush on her cheeks. And those incredible eyes. At first, he'd thought her eyes were blue. At closer range, they were a gorgeous, smoky gray.

"I'm a fixer."

"I don't require fixing, but thanks." He suppressed a smile at the trace of rebelliousness and curiosity warring across her attractive features. Her slender fingers fluttered, and she bent to tug on the hem of her snug fitting jeans. They enhanced the slim curves he'd been admiring for the past hour.

"A business problem is easy to resolve," he continued. "Mine is personal and heart-wrenching."

"Men don't often use the word heart-wrenching."

"I believe heart-wrenching is two words."

She laughed. "It's a relief to meet a sensitive man who is comfortable describing his emotions."

He nodded to the stable. "I'm not all that comfortable."

"Will I have a weeping man at my feet because of a horse?"

His gaze shifted to her. "Nope, although you may have a man sprinting away from a charging horse."

"You harbor many misconceptions about horses."

"Realities," he corrected.

"Yet you allow your daughter to ride."

"Honeycrisp is a pony as you've kindly explained, and Megan's sessions are the result of our doctor's recommendation."

"Well, you enlisted the expertise of a wise doctor." Belle shuffled her feet. She was petite and trim, reminding him of a nimble gymnast. "At any rate, I'm sorry for prying."

"You're young," he said.

She blinked. "What does that have to do with—" Her chin lifted. "I'm almost thirty."

"You're not married."

"I was, for a brief spell."

"Therefore, you're divorced?"

"Yes. He …he left me."

"Why would a man leave a beautiful, empathetic woman like you?"

She shook her head. "Wow. Mr. Bransfield … Andrew … our conversation is becoming too personal."

"I'm forty."

"Thanks for the information, but I don't remember asking your age."

"I'm also divorced. Thus, I have a decade of experience on you."

She pulled blue-rimmed sunglasses from her denim pocket and wiped off the dust. "Perhaps in years."

"But not wisdom?" He waited for a reaction and was rewarded with her tinkling laugh.

"Because you're older, you assume you're more knowledgeable?"

"That's the way it usually works."

"What can you fix, Mr. Knowledgeable?"

"Personally or professionally?"

"Personally."

"Evidently, not much." His gaze rested on her face. "The Scots have a saying, 'Ye'ill dee a thousand deaths ye'ill never see.'"

She quirked a delicate eyebrow. "Please explain the meaning?"

"Don't concern yourself with fixing others."

"Are you sharing your older, better informed advice?"

Something about her teasing voice and pure gray eyes stirred the ashes of his loneliness.

"Yes."

"Mr. Bransfield, not only is our conversation becoming too philosophical for such a lovely day, but you're beginning to sound a lot like my Aunt Lucinda."

"I hope I don't look like her."

"You don't." She chuckled. "My aunt wears a cobalt-blue beret, and her white hair hangs to her shoulders." Belle fidgeted with her sunglasses. "In any event, I've had an upsetting morning and didn't intend to take it out on you."

A breeze ruffled dark-brown wisps from her ponytail. In the shimmering sunlight, she brushed a fine strand from her cheeks. He had the urge to stroke her hair gently, as if she were a precious bird.

Because he felt something. And so did she. He'd felt it in town when they'd locked gazes. And he felt it now.

"Your apology is accepted, though you deserve clarification about my circumstances." He folded his hands together. "Rowena, my ex-wife, never returns my phone calls. As usual, I'd left several messages for her."

"She must be busy."

"She's not busy. She's selfish."

"It's not my place, but perhaps you'd feel better if you didn't judge her."

"Now *you're* becoming too philosophical. When you saw

me, I had walked onto my balcony to breathe in some fresh air."

"I crave fresh air when I'm upset too," Belle said softly.

As if on cue, a delicate breeze rustled the leaves of a nearby Elm tree. More strands flew across her cheeks, and he resisted the urge to brush them away by keeping his hands at his sides.

"I had phoned my ex to inform her that Megan wouldn't be needing surgery," he said.

"Such wonderful news."

He'd conversed with Belle for fifteen minutes, but there was something about her easy-going nature that gave him comfort. She seemed genuinely interested in Megan.

"The patch will come off within a few weeks," he said. "Then she'll be fitted with eyeglasses. When she gets older, she can wear contact lenses if she prefers."

"I've prayed for her full recovery."

"Prayers are always appreciated."

Their gazes stayed connected, and Belle wiped a bead of sweat from her forehead. Scents of sunshine and leather, with an undertone of interest, held them together. Or rather, it held him, for Belle had turned toward the stable.

He wavered. Should he call out to her?

Earlier, when he'd pulled into Candee's driveway, he'd intended to drop off Megan at the riding ring, say hello to Candee and Teddy, and return to his SUV to resume a lengthy list of important business calls to secure new clients.

Besides, horses weren't his thing. They were, as he'd remarked, big. As a rule, he didn't like animals in general.

After he'd met and talked with Belle, though, he'd leaned against the fence and set down his briefcase.

He'd been impressed by her in action. Her silky hair was pulled back into a severe ponytail, and her worn jeans and denim shirt showed off her flawless curves.

She'd walked quietly beside his daughter as she completed the therapy session, talking encouragingly, and he'd hardly noticed when Candee had come to stand beside him. Often when Belle spoke, Megan had giggled. And his heart had swelled. Since his ex-wife's abrupt departure, laughter had been infrequent in the Bransfield household.

He'd been overly involved with dwelling on the hurt she'd caused him and their daughter. As a result, he'd concentrated on his work, allotting precious few occasions for fun. Or joy. Resentment was more comfortable.

"Is there anything else, Mr. Bransfield?" Belle glanced at him. "Megan likes to spend time with Honeycrisp after her therapy sessions, and I left a few treats for the horses."

He still stood in the ring, staring at Belle like a besotted fool.

"Andrew," he reminded with a sardonic smile. "And there is no hurry."

Except for that lengthy list of business calls, though he'd forgotten why they were so important.

Yes, he wanted something else from Belle. He wanted to get to know her better, although why that particular thought floated through his mind was beyond him. The petite dark-haired beauty—who couldn't be any taller than five feet, nor weigh more than a hundred pounds—was stunning. How did she manage those one thousand-pound horses with such ease?

"Miss Belle ... I'm not sure how to address you."

She came around to face him. "Just call me Belle."

"What is your last name?" He studied her delicate hands as she plucked a package of what resembled baby wipes from a backpack, then wiped the dust and grime from a saddle.

"Leather wipes," she explained at his questioning gaze.

He nodded. "Your last name?" he inquired again.

She coupled her hesitation with an awkward, indrawn breath. "Boots."

Andrew lifted his eyebrows. "Your name is Belle Boots?"

A telltale flush heightened her high cheekbones, and she smiled. "I know, I know. It's a ridiculous name for a woman in the equine therapy profession. Belle Boots."

"It's my turn to apologize." He chuckled—he couldn't help it—and was grateful when she joined in. "It's just that you work with horses—"

Her smiled widened, enhancing full, heart-shaped lips. Another attractive feature. "What if my parents had named me Bronco?"

"Bronco Boots," he said easily, "has a nice ring."

"Or Bridle Boots."

"Or Bucking Boots."

She laughed. She had a wry sense of humor, coupled with the ability to joke about herself. Few people were prepared to do that.

"Please accept my compliments on the fine job you're doing with Megan. Did I tell you that already?" He motioned Belle to the railing again. He wished to continue conversing with her, although he was keeping her from her tasks.

"Not in so many words," she replied. "But thank you."

"My daughter has blossomed these past few months." He slipped behind the gate—one never knew when a horse might bound in from the pasture.

"Any credit goes to Megan and Honeycrisp. Their hard work and effort paid off." Belle made a show of shaking the dirt off her brown Western boots—first one boot, then the other. "Megan's face lights up whenever she's riding, which brings me tremendous satisfaction."

In an instant, Andrew relived his daughter's appointments and the trauma she'd undergone—the lighted magnifying glass the doctor had used, the eye drops to blur the vision of the strong eye, the pictures and letter exams when she'd been younger.

"Me too." He swallowed the lump in his throat. He always choked up when he spoke of her welfare.

Certainly, society deemed it acceptable for a man to cry, he'd often told himself.

But was it acceptable?

He'd never seen a grown man cry. None ... except himself.

Surely not his overbearing father.

Rowena had seized on Andrew's perceived weakness and found endless opportunities to chide him. He'd always felt like he was on the outside looking in, anyway.

"Mr. Bransfield," Belle began.

"Andrew."

"Your nanny has referred to you as Mr. Bransfield so often that it's difficult for me to make the transition."

"I'll correct you every time."

"Considerate of you," Belle said wryly.

He smiled. "Although I'm biased because I'm her father, Megan is a delight. Her mother doted on Megan—until she drove off with the delivery man."

Belle's thoughtful expression changed to surprise. "You're joking."

His gaze restlessly shifted to the pasture, then Belle. "Such a cliché, but it's true."

Although he and Rowena had reached a divorce agreement before she'd left because fidelity had never been Rowena's strong suit. He grimaced at the understatement.

That was the thing about a woman as pampered and beautiful as Rowena. She'd demanded only the best, which included a red sports car easily reaching eighty miles an hour in mere seconds. Fast cars and a fast life that had ended with a fast departure.

He trained his gaze on Belle's small hands; she was clutching such an enormous horse's saddle.

"Andrew." Another hesitation. "I'm glad I finally met you."

"We've established this."

"Normally your daughter's nanny brings her to the sessions."

"Nancy, and I'm aware of that fact because I pay her."

"Yes, Nancy," Belle agreed. "Anyway, Megan's sessions with me are coming to an end."

"Really? Why?"

"I'm moving."

He jerked back. The stable, the focal point of his gaze while he stared past Belle, was not lost on her.

"When were you planning on sharing this little tidbit of information?" he asked.

"I didn't intend to withhold anything. I considered emailing you since I just found out this morning. In all fairness, I'm still reeling from the news myself."

"Isn't the decision to move yours?"

"Yes and no. Circumstances happened without warning and prompted me to make a hasty decision." Belle hung the saddle on the fence railing with quick, efficient movements. "I'm relocating to Wilmington. Candee found me an apartment near the beach, on a small farm with a stable. I thought she may have told you when you two were talking."

"Nope. We discussed other things."

"Her barbecue this evening?"

"Yes. Are you going?"

"I can't spare the evening." She sighed. "Unfortunately, I have a bag of potatoes that will go to waste."

"Neither can I." With a dry grin, he added, "No potatoes, though."

Those 'other things' had centered around Megan before he'd asked about Belle. The conversation had ended when the therapy session finished, which was sooner than he'd anticipated.

"Naturally, I will miss your daughter desperately," Belle was saying.

"Then why leave?"

"It's time." Conflicting reactions flickered across her lovely face. "However, my stable in Wilmington needs extensive renovation."

"As well as your apartment?"

"Yes, if the photos are any indication. Fortunately, Candee insisted that Teddy's crew will repair everything for a nominal fee."

He shook his head. "This is a lot to take in."

"Teddy is more than generous."

"I wasn't referring to Teddy's generosity. We've been acquainted for years through our business connections, and he's reliable and honest." Andrew displayed an engaging smile while he assembled a plan. "Exactly when are you leaving?"

"By the end of the month. I'll transport my horse, Jenkins, who is quite nervous. Hopefully, he won't fly into a sweaty panic when he's trailered and—"

"Miss Belle, you're moving?" Megan raced up to them. Wide-eyed, she lifted her freckled face to Belle.

"Yes, and I'm sorry, Megan," Belle said. "I'll miss you very, very much."

"Why are you moving?" The little girl's bottom lip trembled. His daughter's pink cherubic lips were a clear indicator of her distress. As Andrew gazed down at her, timeworn anxieties clustered in his mind. She was still a child, and he intended to shield her from life's disappointments.

"My landlord raised my rent to a rate higher than I can manage," Belle said. "Plus, Wilmington is my hometown, and my aunt lives there."

Megan's shoulders crumpled. "You mean I won't ever see you again?"

"We'll only live a few hours apart. I promise I'll visit Roses whenever possible."

The child balled her tiny hands into fists. She did that, Andrew noted, not in anger, but in frustration whenever she was upset. Now, with Rowena gone, Megan's frustration level had escalated. Again, Andrew was thankful for the equine therapy.

"What about Honeycrisp?" Megan asked.

"I'm certain Honeycrisp can continue to board here," Belle said. "There's no reason why not—"

"As it so happens, Belle," Andrew broke in, "I'll renovate your stable at no charge."

She was a bargain-hunter, right? Anyone who fretted about wasting a bag of potatoes wouldn't be able to resist his offer.

"Thank you, but Teddy's crewmen will provide the repairs," she replied.

"Yes, so you mentioned." He greeted her reply with all the enthusiasm of a root canal. "How's this?"

"How's what?"

"I'll renovate at *no* charge, including the work on your apartment." His competitiveness kicked in. Why not? The trait had contributed to his company's significant success. However, he was in the business of making money, not losing it. Therefore, providing a service and materials without payment was not a keen business practice.

Nonetheless, he was significantly more interested in Belle Boots than any monetary gain. Surely she couldn't resist the rock-bottom offer of a lifetime. Nothing beat free.

"Thank you." Belle looked away. "Still, I can't accept your kindness. We are hardly acquainted, and it wouldn't be right."

Her response only encouraged him.

Lightly, he placed his hand on her shoulder. "Considering all you've done for my daughter, most definitely you can consent. I'm expanding my company, Bransfield Designs, to Wilmington. Moreover, I've considered purchasing a beach house and residing near the sea with Megan in a calm, relaxing little place. Maybe I'll rent the house when we're not there."

He did? Since when? He didn't have a second to cavort on a beach or deal with renters—not with his schedule.

"We're moving to be near Miss Belle, Daddy?" Megan perked up as she tugged on his shirtsleeve.

"We're flitting to live closer to the ocean."

"Flitting?" Belle inquired.

"A Scottish term for moving. We'll use the house on holidays." He lifted Megan onto his shoulders. "You like the beach, don't you?"

She clapped her hands together. "I love the beach!"

He swung toward Belle. "What say you, Miss Belle Boots?"

"I've never been the object of a bidding war. Are you certain Teddy won't mind?"

"I'll tell him myself. No worries."

Belle smiled. "What about you, Andrew?"

"What about me?"

"Do *you* like the beach?"

"Doesn't everyone?" His lips twitched. "Oceanside living, dining on fresh caught fish, surfing …"

"You fish?"

"Nope."

"Surf?"

"Never."

They shared a chuckle.

Quiet walks on the sand with Belle accompanied by a

chirpy Megan gathering seashells. He grinned inwardly at the agreeable prospect.

"Megan and I will appreciate a change of scenery and an opportunity to escape the sweltering summers in town. A beach house where we can savor sunsets and watch the tide roll in."

"Savor sunsets?" Belle chuckled. "You are a remarkably poetic man."

"Sensitive," he corrected, planting a kiss on Megan's chubby leg. "Blame it on my Scottish ancestry. We Scots are a thoughtful people."

"Don't forget stubborn," Belle quipped.

He laughed. "You've been watching too much Braveheart."

"I've never seen the movie."

"Someday, we'll watch it together."

"The movie is about Scotland's history, right?"

"Somewhat." He combined his shrug with a grin and his shoulders relaxed. The pleasant mood was a respite from his usual tenseness "The cinematography is stunning."

He and Megan deserved peace and closure, he rationalized. A beach house was the ticket, along with the opportunity to see the lovely Belle. Yet, actually finding the perfect house would involve an experienced Realtor who acted quickly.

As he set Megan down, she turned her face to his. "Daddy, can Honeycrisp move with us to Wilmington?"

"Absolutely. Perhaps we can board Honeycrisp at Miss Belle's new stable." He smiled and met Belle's gaze. "Obviously, I'll pay the usual boarding rate."

"Do you have any idea what that is, Andrew?"

"Candee charges six hundred dollars a month. I expect you'll charge me a fair price as well."

"Rest assured, considering your free labor." Warily, she regarded him.

"So." He displayed his most charismatic smile, "I assume everything is agreed, then, right?"

CHAPTER 3

*S*omehow, this entire situation seemed mildly unethical, Belle mused, as she gazed at the two horses in her newly renovated stable in Wilmington. In record time, Andrew had enlisted a crew. They'd completely gutted the stable—replacing the tack, feed rooms, and wash stalls. After installing the latest lighting and a septic system, she'd opted for sliding stall doors and a concrete floor. The damaged fence lines had been repaired, as well as the post gate's hinge.

She might be a bargain hunter, but when it came to her horses, she never scrimped.

Straightaway, Andrew had notified Teddy that he was taking over "Belle's Project." From her conversation with Candee, Belle learned that Andrew and Megan had moved into a two-story oceanfront beach house.

In the month since, Andrew's crewmen had transported Honeycrisp to Belle's stable, and the gentle pony now had the finicky Jenkins as a neighboring stall mate.

Belle had ensured that a bag of Honeycrisp's feed was available, and hand walked the horse around the fence line in an effort to ease her into the different environment. Systematically, she familiarized Honeycrisp with the pasture. Once she was stalled, Honeycrisp and Jenkins eyed each other at a distance. After a few days, Belle turned them out together in the pasture, placing their feed over a large space with ample room around the water source. Sure, there'd been some biting and chasing—mostly by Jenkins, because he hadn't been thrilled with the situation.

Fortunately, both horses had ultimately settled into a contented routine.

In a flurry of busyness, Belle had moved her belongings into her sunlit and welcoming new apartment. Boasting a wide, fully equipped breakfast area, an adjoining living room with a pull-out couch, and a small bedroom with an attached bathroom, it was upscale and chic. She was impressed by the renovation, scarcely believing the home was now hers.

Through numerous texts, Andrew had inquired about her vision for a dream kitchen and she had described espresso cabinets, stainless steel appliances and wood-style flooring. After hand-sketching the design and emailing her for approval, he'd taken her words to heart and delivered to the letter.

Thrilled to discover her place was a mere six blocks from the ocean, she jogged on the beach every morning and again at sundown.

As always she woke at dawn, showered, dressed and went to the stable. She opened the door, and both horses stuck their heads out of their stalls to greet her. She fed them grain in a bucket, distributed the hay, and cleaned and refilled the water buckets. After brushing their coats and applying fly spray, she haltered and walked the horses to the pasture.

Chores came next, which began with sweeping the stalls.

Once finished, she hiked through an overgrown shortcut to the beach, removed her waterproof muck boots and jogged barefoot along the shore. The soothing splash of water on her toes brought her spirits up. Surely, she'd made the right decision in relocating to Wilmington.

Her eccentric Aunt Lucinda had been thrilled Belle was back in their hometown, and Belle visited her often. Her aunt had never married, spouting that a man would tie her down. Nevertheless, there had been one man in her life, she'd confessed. A man she'd loved, although she'd never divulged his name.

Men were too much of a bother, she'd stated on numerous occasions.

After her divorce from Tyler, Belle had agreed. Nevertheless, after numerous hours talking and texting with Andrew, she'd changed her mind. He displayed a kindness, courteousness, and indisputable attentiveness that proved both disarming and heartening.

With a tremulous smile, she recalled their initial meeting. Apprehension had been written across his handsome features when he'd surveyed Blackjack and Honeycrisp. Just wait until he came face-to-face with the cantankerous Jenkins. She'd need to introduce them gently.

After her jog, Belle returned to the stable. She intended to clean the hay out of the stalls, replace old tack, and carry out the million other chores awaiting her.

Tires crunching on gravel prompted her to shade her eyes and peer toward the road, as Andrew drove into the driveway in his shiny silver SUV.

He got out of the SUV and strode to her with a decidedly mischievous grin. He wore slim jeans, a white T-shirt that clung to his broad shoulders and work boots. In one hand, he carried a toolbox.

Her heart did a thump.

He looked entirely different from the fine-looking professional of a few weeks ago.

Because today, wearing jeans and a T-shirt?

Oh, my.

The morning at Candee's stable he'd been pin-striped proper, and Belle couldn't choose which look she preferred.

The jeans, she decided. Definitely the jeans.

"Hi, Andrew." She smiled as he neared.

"Greetings, Belle." He withdrew a bouquet of slightly wilted yellow flowers from his toolbox.

To discount the treacherous jump of her heart, she tried to think of something to say. "Tools and flowers," she observed. *Just brilliant, Belle.*

"Do you like flowers?" he asked.

"I love flowers, and the color reminds me of a burst of sunshine."

"I like flowers too. However, the tools aren't for you. Only the flowers. When I passed by the florist in town, I thought, 'Beautiful flowers for a beautiful woman' and I couldn't resist. What's more, they were on sale, so I knew you'd approve."

"I hope they were at least fifty percent off?"

"Try a dollar off."

"What was the original price?"

"Fifty dollars."

"What?" Raising a hand, she checked him from continuing. "You paid forty-nine dollars for a bouquet?"

He bent to nuzzle her ear and whispered, "For you, I would have paid a hundred dollars."

She couldn't contain her grin.

He liked flowers. He liked *her.* And he was a wonderful father. Contrary to his rugged exterior, he possessed a sensitive nature. She wondered if he wrote poetry.

Probably.

"Thank you." She accepted the bouquet and sniffed.

"Flowers as pretty as dahlias should have a strong, fragrant scent, but they don't."

"We think alike. I told the florist the same thing."

"They're gorgeous."

"They're a house-warming gift."

"You didn't have to do this."

"I wanted to."

Her cheeks heated beneath his steady, admiring gaze. "You've done too much already."

"You've heard the familiar adage." He finger quoted. "'It's better to give than to receive.'"

"You mean, there's no Scottish saying?"

"'Don't judge each day by the harvest you reap, but by the seeds you plant.'"

She plucked a petal from the dahlia's stem. "That's Scottish?"

"By Scotland's very own novelist, Robert Louis Stevenson."

"Which I assume means, 'It's better to give than to get?'"

"Nope." Unabashed, he chuckled. "Sadly, it's the best I can come up with."

She placed the bouquet in a shady area. "You knew my favorite flower?"

"I asked Candee, and she mentioned your former apartment was painted yellow. Thus, I selected dahlias."

"Most people think of daisies for a yellow flower."

"I studied the meanings of both. In our situation, dahlias were more appropriate."

She made a mental note to research the meanings. "Andrew Bransfield, you're an extraordinarily thoughtful man."

He nodded. "I also was compelled to see if the stable area begs for my finishing touches."

"No begging is required." She gestured to the fencing. "Thanks to you, every inch is repaired."

He eyed the pasture where the two horses sunbathed. "Are they safe?"

"Do you mean, are we safe from them?"

"Both."

"We are all safe and secure," she said.

He set down the toolbox. "Just in case, I'll keep a safe and secure distance from them."

"Why are you afraid of horses?"

"When I was young, I was attacked by a large dog and required stitches."

"I'm sorry." She paused, picked up a rake and piled dry straw into mounds. "That must have been frightening."

"It was traumatic for a ten-year-old kid who loved animals."

"Past tense?" she inquired. "*Loved* animals?"

He shrugged. "I suppose."

She let the comment pass. It wasn't the time to analyze him. "What type of dog attacked you?"

"If you're suspecting a mean, vicious dog, you're wrong. The day was scorching, the hottest on record, and I ran up to the dog to pet him. His name was Rusty, and he belonged to a neighbor. Apparently, I startled him, and he bit me." Andrew pointed to a thin white line on his forearm. "Consequently, animals aren't my number one love."

What was his number one love?

Without a doubt, it was Megan. His devotion to his daughter was undeniable.

"I guarantee you're safe from any galloping horses," Belle said.

"Whew!" He forced a larger-than-life wipe at his forehead, but his posture tensed as his gaze canvassed the pasture. "Are you certain?"

"Totally." She decided to hold off telling him that a stray tabby had found his way to her front yard and she'd immediately adopted and dubbed him Ginger. Or about the two white goats, Hester and Hilda, who were already members of the farm when she'd showed up.

Andrew would find out soon enough.

He paused and gazed at her. "You are gorgeous, Belle," he said quietly.

Donned in a pair of military-green cropped pants and a striped crewneck shirt, she highly doubted it. She opened her mouth to dispute him, but he forestalled her by leaning over the fence and gently sliding a finger across her lips.

His touch was casual and friendly and brought an unexpected tingle. Dumbstruck, she shook her head at the strong attraction.

"Sorry." He dropped his hand. "Did I invade your personal space?"

Not a bit, she wished to tell him, but refrained from speaking.

She returned to tackling the raking with outward efficiency, though her fingers trembled so significantly she could hardly hold the rake. She gave up, set the rake down and glanced at her watch. "Are you on a lunch break, Andrew?"

He gestured to his jeans. "Does it look like I am?"

"No, but it's Friday. We've texted often enough for me to be aware of your grueling schedule."

His green eyes sparkled with laughing speculation. "What might my grueling schedule entail?"

"At seven a.m. you eat breakfast with Megan. Once her nanny arrives, you report to your office by eight. You allot a half hour for lunch and leave work by six in order to spend an hour with Megan before her bedtime."

"If I'm lucky. I wish I had more time," came his frustrated reply.

"Oftentimes you take your computer home," she went on. "And I know you're up at all hours of the night, because I've received texts from you at three a.m. asking which flooring style I prefer."

"You've memorized my schedule in only a few short weeks."

"You're easy because your routine is always the same. Work, work, work." She tried a lame attempt at sternness. "Any robber could watch you for a couple days and then fleece you blind."

He grinned, but his eyes darkened, reminding her of pine trees in the subdued light of a summer sunset.

"Are you planning to rob me, Belle? Of my senses, perhaps? Because I lose track of time when I'm with you. In fact, I'm not certain of anything since we met."

Surely he joked. They were business acquaintances. Yet he sounded surprisingly off balance. Seeking to lighten the strangely intimate mood, she said, "You certainly lost your senses when you offered your services for free."

"Let's not forget my phone and text consultations."

"Is there an added fee?"

"Certainly."

"We talked about other matters," she reminded.

The way he watched her filled her with compassion and affection. Although business had dominated their exchanges, he'd spoken about his daughter and the challenges he'd encountered upon becoming a single parent. His intent was to make everything right in his daughter's world, he'd said. Or rather, it seemed, he was bent on make everything right in the *entire* world.

When silence had rung out, he'd encouraged Belle to discuss her reservations regarding her relocation and leaving behind her clients. She felt as though she had abandoned them.

Andrew had immediately corrected her when she had used the term "abandon," and she could almost see him visibly flinch. "You're a kind, caring woman," he'd declared, and her refutes were no match against his thoughtful assurances.

Belle grabbed the rake again and swirled the dry grass round and round. She concentrated on the areas near the gate that got the highest traffic. When Andrew stayed silent, she motioned to the stable. "Are your rates generally expensive, then?"

His dark eyebrows rose in a teasing challenge. "Extremely."

"Could I afford you if you charged me your regular fee?"

"Highly doubtful."

Their laughing gazes joined.

"In truth, helping you was my pleasure," Andrew said softly.

She slanted him a glance and yanked up a garden hose to water the riding ring.

Andrew held up his hands. "Do you intend to spray me, Belle?"

Hmm. No. Or maybe?

"Push the notion from your mind." He retreated a step. "We are both adults, and a prank like the one you're thinking would be extremely childish."

"How do you know what I'm thinking?"

"I just know."

"And why should I obey you?"

"Because I asked politely."

"Politeness only goes so far, Andrew." She inched closer to him and unlatched the gate. Sunlight glinted through his hair, lightening the shade to a shiny copper penny.

He refused to retreat any further. Her beating heart brought a knot of longing and indescribable attraction. Now? Yes, now. It had been years since her divorce. Although she wasn't actively searching for a relationship, she appreciated the company of a good-hearted, kind man. A man who laughed at silly pranks. A man with substance and confidence.

"The hose?" he reminded. "You're aiming at me rather than the ground."

"What's more, I'll continue aiming at you until you admit you lead a highly regimented life."

"Where did that come from?" She expected him to take flight, but he held his ground. "Is this truth or dare?"

"Possibly," she hedged.

"I'm a businessman." He shrugged with an indifference Belle suspected was partly feigned. "Need I explain more?"

"Yes." With an innocent smile, she turned the hose on him.

CHAPTER 4

*a*ndrew toppled backwards and landed on the grass while Belle's chuckle pealed through the air.

He peered at his wet shirt then up at her. "Was that necessary?"

She dropped the hose and hurried over, taking stock of him sprawled on the ground. "Was it necessary for you to display such an ambitious dramatization?"

"I was startled."

"Uh huh. You're hardly wet."

"I'm wet enough."

Her gaze narrowed. "Aren't you getting up?"

"Maybe."

She came to stand over him. "Time to get up," she repeated.

"Why?" he countered. "Are you standing by to spray me again?"

"Maybe." She repaid his question with uncharacteristic sarcasm. Belatedly registering his frown, she guardedly asked, "Are you hurt?"

"Only my pride. Fortunately, I have a thick skin in my business." His tone sounded forced despite his assertion, bringing an ache to her throat. She considered his wet shirt, and regretted spraying him. What had seemed like a fun, playful idea a few seconds earlier now wasn't quite as humorous.

He was under obvious emotional strain, trying to keep his architectural firm prosperous while spending considerable time with his daughter. Which was the very reason why she'd injected light-heartedness into their morning. That, and the fact he'd given her the idea. Why, he'd practically goaded her.

Now, seeing him defenseless, the solemn expression on his ruggedly handsome face caused her pulse to quiver. He had a mysterious effect on her she couldn't shake, whether he was upright or on the ground.

Her memory of him when he'd strode onto his balcony flashed through her mind. She remembered thinking how pleasingly male he looked, so urbane in his sophisticated home. The fact that his ex-wife had brought such sorrow to him and his little girl prompted Belle's empathy.

His skin might be thick in business, but he was an exceptional breed—emotional and vulnerable while exuding a tough exterior.

He continued to lie in the grass. He was either milking the situation or trying to tug at her heart strings. He accomplished both quite successfully.

If, indeed, the force of the water had knocked him off his feet.

"I apologize," she began offering him the benefit of the doubt. "You're right. That was childish of me."

"I accept." He squinted up at her, shielding his eyes from the sun. "That is, unless you're planning to hose me again?"

She held out a hand to help him to his feet. "I hardly call dampening your shirt hosing you down."

With an overstated sigh, he stood and brushed the grass

sticking to his white shirt. He'd have grass stains, which were difficult to wash out, but she didn't tell him that.

"I brought no change of clothes," he said.

"With the hot July sun beating down, your shirt will dry in five minutes," she assured.

Together, they walked back to the riding ring holding hands.

There, she paused to consider the fencing. "Thank you for combining wire mesh along with the wood. As I explained, otherwise horses might catch their legs. Plus the fence is more resilient."

"Are you always this conscientious, Belle?" he asked.

"I've lived around horses and pastures since I was a teen. Fencing and barns come with the territory."

"Both are alien territories to me."

"Because you sit in an office all day."

"You're a master at describing me, but could you toss in a few descriptions other than businessman now and then? I'm an architect and work outdoors often. While we're discussing the subject, let's not forget *you're* a businesswoman."

"I'm proud of the distinction." Her dignified reproof brought a grin to his lips. "Studies prove professional women are more emotionally intelligent than men."

His steady, green-eyed gaze met hers. "Please continue."

They still held hands. He didn't seem to want to let go. Neither did she.

"Well," she adopted a formidable instructor's manner, "a woman values a person's well-being."

"And I don't?"

"You're taking my words personally. I was comparing men to women—not all men in general."

They reached the spot where she'd dropped the hose. He

released her hand, eyed the hose and grinned. Quietness billowed between them.

"Therefore, I'm not necessarily referring to you," she clarified.

"It's important to spell out the difference."

"I did." She tilted her head and granted a genuine smile. "Furthermore, women aren't as ego-driven as men."

"I agree that men like to win." Still grinning, Andrew grabbed the hose, held steady, and aimed at her.

She gaped, steering away from the sudden stream of gushing water. "You, Mr. Bransfield, are incorrigible," she shouted.

He shut the hose. "Did I win?"

"Definitely not. And because of you, my hair will stick out straight the rest of the day."

"Your hair will dry in a few minutes. Remember? The hot sun and all that ..." He gestured upward to the airy white clouds floating in a blue sky.

She ran a hand through her hair, squeezing the ends with her fingers. Helplessly, she laughed. "If you even consider turning that hose on me again ..."

In three quick strides, he reached her. "Do you give up easily?"

"Never." With a cool dose of spitfire, she included, "Unless this is a water fight."

"It may yet become one."

"Andrew ... don't you dare ..."

"Now I'm Andrew again? Which is it, Belle? Mr. Bransfield or Andrew?"

"I told you already. Because your nanny referred to you as Mr. Bransfield so often—"

"You and I have progressed to a first name basis since then."

"Are you asking a question?" She shied backward. She was

ready for the game to end, especially while he still held the hose.

"It's a statement." He looked positively boyish, a sparkling gleam in his eyes as he set down the hose. "And I promise I won't spray you again under one condition."

"Now there's a condition?"

In reply, his laughter was deep and intimate. His gaze fell to her lips.

She drew a shaky inhale. They stood within inches of each other.

"What is the condition?" she asked again.

"This." Tenderly, he brushed his knuckles across her cheek, outlined her lips with his fingertips. The rhythm in her veins accelerated, taking on a mind of its own as he bent his head and kissed her.

She melted, responding to the radiant heat of his mouth as he drew her into his arms. Her heart beat much too fast, but in that moment she was aware of only one thing.

She'd been waiting for his kiss, anticipating it. He'd been waiting too. She had seen the desire in his gaze, heard the underlying huskiness.

When had their magnetism begun? In Roses?

Or here? In Wilmington?

He framed her face and deepened the kiss.

No, no, no.

But she couldn't surface from the delicious pleasure of his lips.

She slid her hands around his neck and kissed him back, reacting to the instinctive tightening of his arms as he brought her tightly against him. So close, she felt the beating of his heart.

When he loosened his hold, she leaned against the fence until their breathing slowed. After a lingering silence, he said softly, "I've had an urge to kiss you ever since we met."

"You evidently have no objections to personal space," she half-joked.

"None at all." His voice quieted. "Not when it comes to you."

How should she respond? Start with the truth. Confess she had the same feelings.

Absolutely not, that would never do. A woman shouldn't wear her heart on her sleeve.

She swallowed. When she was with him, she was vaguely aware that she was negotiating a land mine, with no relationship experience to guide her except for a degrading ex and a marriage that never should have happened.

Andrew, on the other hand, with his charisma-plus charm and velvety Scottish lilt, left her no choice but to examine each of her words, because to say exactly what she thought and describe her emotions would expose her. She was attracted to him, very attracted, but it was too soon in their friendship for those thoughts.

This was merely a kiss between a man and a woman who had worked together the past few weeks and had become close.

Andrew appeared to take the change in their relationship with an easy-going stride. His face was calm, his features neutral.

"You're getting off the hook easily with your personal space reply, if that sums up your explanation," she said shakily.

"With you, all bets are off." He chuckled when she frowned. "Belle, you are beautiful and desirable. Be proud of that." When she continued frowning, he chuckled louder. "You know, there is simply no substitute for a smart, perceptive businesswoman."

With a self-conscious laugh, she didn't refute him. Unfortunately, her conscience deemed this as the appropriate time for an admonition.

Remember? Andrew was the father of one of her clients.

Should she have accepted his help so willingly? Or kissed him? Their association was professional, not personal.

Yet, Andrew had done more for her than anyone.

How could she repay him? Everything—materials and labor—is free of charge, he'd insisted. In the short weeks they'd been acquainted, he'd proven a wonderful friend.

Friend, she reminded herself.

He had the resources, restating that this was his opportunity to repay the kindness, patience, and understanding she'd shown his daughter.

She stood motionless. Hesitant to speak, hesitant not to speak.

Andrew broke the silence by fixing his thumbs in his pockets and stepping away. "Back to business," he remarked.

No beat was missed. He bent to inspect the fence, tugged on the gate, and began measuring the replaced wood.

He hadn't dismissed her, had he?

"Business as usual," she echoed. She wished her voice sounded as unshaken as his. "Are you resuming duty as my project foreman?"

"I never went off duty."

Sure he had, when he'd kissed her a moment earlier, but some thoughts weren't meant to be shared.

He cleared his throat. "Is everything falling into place the way you imagined?"

At the stable? Unquestionably.

In the heart department? She wasn't so certain.

He pulled a hammer and nails from the toolbox and secured a piece of wire mesh to the fencing.

"I love this area. It's my hometown," she began answering

his question. She stifled the urge to gush on and on about herself. "How about you and *your* new place?"

"Couldn't be better. I'm delighted with the house now that Megan and I are mostly unpacked."

"Where is Megan? I meant to inquire when you arrived."

"Her nanny took her to play on the beach."

"Nancy?"

"I hired Adella, a new nanny, and I'll rehire Nancy if Megan and I return to Roses."

If.

Was he thinking of settling in Wilmington indefinitely?

"I mentioned Adella to you the other day," he was saying.

He had, she admitted to him. In the torrent of activity, she'd forgotten.

"Megan will begin again soon, right?" he asked.

"I scheduled her on Monday. I'm looking forward to our weekly sessions because I've missed her."

"Excellent." His mouth tilted up whenever he spoke of his daughter. "She misses you too and mentions you constantly."

During Belle's move, Andrew had texted or phoned often. There was an easiness about conversing with him behind a safe screen which had served as a safety net. However, communicating in person was something else entirely. Suddenly feeling awkward, she drew up the rake and concentrated on a rutted area.

"Do you like your new home?" she inquired.

"Very much. Thanks to our super Realtor friend, Candee, my house is in a secluded area by the ocean. Megan and I will invite you for dinner some night. Our evenings are quiet and lonely."

Somehow, watching this undeniably compelling man, she sincerely doubted he spent his evenings alone.

"You cook?" she asked.

"My housekeeper does. She is from Scotland."

"I'm not familiar with Scottish food."

"Have you ever eaten haggis?"

"I've never heard of haggis. Is it a variety of sausage?"

"A little more." He chuckled. "My sister, Kate, who lives in Scotland, used to prepare authentic haggis."

"Used to? How long since you've last seen her?"

His features shuttered. "Many years."

"Why? Don't you ever visit Scotland?"

"Kate retained the rights to our ancestral home with my blessings." He crossed his arms over his chest. "Scotland is dead to me."

"You aren't keen on visiting?"

He stepped away, his posture rigid. "Nope."

"How many sisters do you have?"

"Only Kate. As a young boy, I was surrounded by femininity—my mother and several maids, and a wee elipel."

"Meaning?"

"Kate was a tattle-tale."

"You're holding a juvenile grudge against her because of that?"

"I'm not shallow, and this is an adult feud." He propped his elbows on the fence. "You?"

She shook her head. "I'm an only child. Do you have any brothers?"

"No other males aside from my father who was too busy womanizing to take care of his business properly. He couldn't be trusted with holding on to the family fortune."

In the wake of Andrew's unemotional attitude, Belle floundered.

"Both of my parents were domineering and opinionated," she finally said. "Fortunately, my Aunt Lucinda doesn't subscribe to artificiality. She's my mother's sister—spry and wiry and a hoot."

"She lives in Wilmington?"

"Yes. She lives alone, although she traveled the country on a Harley in her younger years. Finally she retired, boasts numerous friends and enjoys entertaining. She is free with her jokes ... and her colorful phrases."

"I'd like to meet her. Her experience and wisdom must span decades."

"It does. Fair warning, though. She narrates her adventures with a larger-than-life laugh." Belle paused to study him. "I wager she'd like to meet you too."

"Thus, we have a date." Before she refuted, he grabbed a handful of nails. "I'll ensure the other side of the fence is solid."

Wait. There was more to discuss, beginning with ... he had an overbearing father?

She counted on Andrew to elaborate, but he apparently didn't wish to discuss his family any further. Only hers. Only work. He had a way of doing that.

After he strode away, Belle pulled out her cellphone.

She discovered that haggis was a national Scottish dish comprised of the liver, heart, and lungs of a sheep. The recipe got better, or worse—depending on a person's appetite—because the mixture was boiled in a sheep's stomach. If haggis was ever on a menu, she'd stick with a more appetizing entrée, such as mashed potatoes and turnips.

She then texted Candee to inquire about Andrew's new house.

Five bedrooms and five bathrooms, including an in-ground pool, came Candee's immediate text. *From the photos, it's spectacular and even boasts an elevator. The address is One Carolina Way.*

Why would he rent such a large home? Belle texted.

The inventory for oceanfront is sparse, and hardly any are available. And he liked the lines.

What does that mean?

Architectural talk, LOL, and the house has an option to buy.

Belle paused. *He's considering purchasing a home in Wilmington?*

Do you realize who he is? He owns Bransfield Designs, the most profitable architectural firm in the Carolinas. Also, he's been praised in numerous magazines as being a creative genius.

No, Belle hadn't realized, although Megan's nanny had mentioned Andrew's firm on occasion.

The creative genius description fit him, though.

"I honestly don't care what people think about me," he'd once said.

And he kept odd hours, sometimes texting her in the middle of the night. When she'd asked when he slept, he'd replied that his mind was always racing.

When it came to his wealth, he paid the monthly invoices for Megan's sessions quickly, which marked the extent of Belle's knowledge regarding Andrew's finances. He owned a grand home in Roses and now rented in Wilmington and employed a nanny and housekeeper.

Thanks, she texted.

Andrew stood at the other end of the fence, scrutinizing and hammering, looking as if he would happily spend the entire afternoon repairing fences.

When she typed his name on the Internet, her jaw literally dropped. He came from a notable line of aristocrats who had resided in the Scottish Highlands. His biography detailed the family's relocation to the United States when Andrew was young because his father's investment business had gone under.

Andrew had attended public schools and there was no mention of college.

A quick scan detailed his propensity for architecture and how he'd begun Bransfield Designs with little capital. Nowadays, he didn't work for professional gain. He was compelled by something else.

A driving force within him he couldn't quell, perhaps? She admired him for making it on his own resolve.

Impressive. Very impressive. That explained his refined jaw, his straight, regal bearing, and her realization that he wasn't a millionaire. Because, in actuality, he was a billionaire.

With a quick mapping she learned he lived a short distance from her apartment, his home located on a private stretch of beach.

She looked up as he ducked into the stable, then quickly exited.

As he advanced toward her, she snapped her cellphone shut and jammed it into her pocket.

"There's a mirror in the horse stall," he said.

"Right."

"Why?"

"Years ago, I rescued Jenkins from a racetrack because he'd been mistreated. Sadly, he fretted about being closed off. Thus I brought in the acrylic mirror for companionship. He's high strung."

"Not only is Jenkins a horse, but he's a high strung horse?"

"He can't help being a horse, and he's rewarded my rescue with affection and loyalty." She gestured at the fencing. "All set?"

"The fence will hold for years. I'm pleased with the work-manship."

"Because you and your crew were responsible for the repairs."

"Something like that." He gave a short laugh. "None-theless, there are always improvements—even for my spec-tacular crewmen."

"Always the perfectionist."

"Does it show?" A sardonic smile tugged at his lips. "By the way, there's another reason I'm here today. I hope to take you to lunch."

And to kiss her.

"I'm flattered," she replied. "I had wondered why you stopped by unexpectedly. I assumed it wasn't solely to bring me flowers."

"A man needs no excuse to gift flowers to a stunning woman. Do you accept my offer?"

"For lunch?" She considered her appearance—jean shorts and a T-shirt, and promptly shook her head. "Unfortunately, I can't."

"Why not?"

"Look around," she averred. *Just look at me.* Her hair was still damp and plastered to her forehead. Any makeup she'd applied that morning, a light peach gloss, had surely disappeared hours ago.

"Can we reschedule?" he asked.

"Feasibly." He looked so disappointed, she supplied, "Although I can whip you up an exquisite omelette. A French omelette, not your run-of-the-mill American-style scrambled eggs."

"What's the difference?"

"Basically the way the eggs are rolled."

"You cook?"

"Not gourmet, but I get by. I'm pretty much an amateur."

"Are you inviting me to lunch?"

"I snagged a great deal on a dozen eggs. What's more, you can inspect the remodel on my apartment. All you've seen up till now are photos."

He smiled. "That being the case, I gladly accept." He gathered his hammer and nails and placed them neatly in his toolbox.

He was clearly a man who didn't object to rolling up his sleeves, working alongside his crewmen, and getting calluses on his hands. He was also equally comfortable in a board room wearing a fine woolen suit.

He directed his gaze toward the pasture. "Are the horses okay if we go inside?"

"On a nice day when the humidity isn't high and there's no rain or bad weather in the forecast, grazing in a pasture is ideal for horses." She lifted an eyebrow. "Why, are you concerned about them?"

"Just wondering."

"One might say you actually like horses."

"One might say you're wrong."

"Despite your reservations, I applaud you for placing the well-being of your daughter before your fears," Belle said. "You allow her to experience the joys of riding. Someday you'll realize that horses are like family. Speaking of Megan, how does she like Wilmington?"

"She met a girl her age who lives nearby. She loves inviting friends over for play dates. She used to be a fun-loving kid. Hopefully, she will again …" He fell silent, but Belle heard the catch in his voice.

He was a father who loved his child.

She nodded. "Are you ready to taste my delectable omelette?"

"More than ready." He bent to pick up his toolbox when Hester bleated, drawing Belle's attention. And, unfortunately, Andrew's as well.

Andrew paused. "What's that?"

Belle slanted him a wry glance. "A goat."

"You mean while I was fixing the fence, that goat was hiding?"

"He wasn't hiding. Hester and Hilda were preoccupied in the patch of woods beyond the stable."

"So while I was feeling safe and secure, I truly wasn't." Cautiously, Andrew peered around. "Hilda? There's a Hilda?"

"A male and a female. Hilda is Hester's sister. To alleviate your concerns, goats are intelligent, gentle creatures."

He scratched his head. "Goats as in plural?"

"I have a little herd of two. Or rather, the farm does. Goats don't like being alone."

Andrew retreated as Hester and Hilda rounded the stable. "What type of goats are they?"

"They're referred to as myotonic goats."

"Will they charge at us?"

"Hester never has. I doubt Hilda will." The air stilled apart from Andrew's quiet, indrawn breath as he suspiciously eyed the two white goats.

"Should I walk carefully?" he asked.

"Definitely, as running or a loud noise will startle them. They might faint."

"Seriously?"

"I couldn't be more serious."

Gingerly, he stepped to his SUV, opened the door, and placed the toolbox on the back seat.

Belle nodded her approval and placed a forefinger to her lips. "We'll walk quietly to my apartment," she whispered.

With a nod, Andrew lifted his foot to close the door. It slammed shut.

Belle jumped.

And the goats fainted.

CHAPTER 5

Comfortably sitting on a stool in Belle's cozy kitchen ten minutes later, Andrew favorably assessed the improvements. The walls were now painted the color of butter, and despite the small size, the breakfast area was expansive. A brilliant yellow cuckoo clock, sporting a bird and leaf motif, recapped the hour with a dual chime.

A sizable granite countertop island separated the kitchen from the living room. Barn-style doors led to the hallway, bathroom, and Belle's bedroom. Wide-plank oak flooring, stainless steel appliances, and a glass tile accent wall enhanced the espresso cabinets.

Once they entered her apartment, they stepped out of their boots. She padded to the kitchen and filled a plain white vase with water, setting the dahlias in the center of the island. Quickly, she'd shown him the apartment.

He pointed to a stain on the hallway ceiling. "There's a roof leak? I presumed we fixed everything."

"Me too. The other day it rained, and I quickly grabbed a bucket. I alerted my landlords, Abby and Felix, but they're a young couple and struggle financially."

"I'll take care of it," Andrew said.

"Thanks." She pinned back her hair and washed her hands at the kitchen sink, requesting he do the same. She tied an apron embossed with lemons around her waist while Andrew texted Adella.

He was reassured that Megan was enjoying a delightful afternoon building a sandcastle in front of their home.

Are you using lots of sunscreen? he asked. He always kept Megan's fair, freckled skin in mind.

She is plastered from head to toe, came the nanny's reply. *Her playmate has joined us.*

Good. He smiled and snapped his phone shut. Yes, a move to Wilmington was definitely in his daughter's best interests.

He gazed at Belle. And his interests, too.

"Is Megan having fun at the beach?" Belle inquired.

"Her nanny said she's loving it."

"Did they go to a Wilmington beach?"

"They're closer to my home."

"Your home is near the beach?"

"It's beachfront."

When she responded with silence, he upbraided himself. He certainly hadn't intended to flaunt his wealth, but in all fairness, Belle was also within walking distance of the beach. His place happened to be oceanfront.

She spread her arms wide. "Your house must cost two thousand dollars a month in rent."

The lease was more like five thousand, but he didn't share that information.

Belle pulled a frying pan from the cabinet and added a pat of butter to the pan to sizzle on the stove while she cracked and beat a half dozen eggs into a mixing bowl.

"Is a cheese omelette okay?" She poured him a glass of her "famous" southern style iced tea from the refrigerator.

"What exactly is southern style iced tea?" he asked.

She set the pitcher on the table. "You live in the south. Don't you know?"

"I'm originally from Scotland."

"You moved to America when you were eighteen."

"Where did you hear that?"

She flushed, which prompted his grin. She'd done her due diligence—perhaps gleaning her information about him from Candee.

"Anyhow, with your Scottish brogue, how can I forget where you're originally from?" She smiled. "Southern iced tea requires heaps of sugar and freshly squeezed lemons. Also, the lemons were on sale."

He grinned and reclaimed the stool. He drained his glass and concluded that sugar was the gateway to happiness. He set down his glass and Belle quickly tipped the pitcher and refilled.

"Did the grocery store offer a deal on cheese this week too, when you went for your messages?" he asked.

"What messages?"

"The Scottish term for groceries."

"You Scots have such interesting words."

He lifted his glass as a salute. "So do you Americans."

"I assume you're American too."

"Yes, I claim dual citizenship, although I haven't been back to Scotland for many years." He surveyed the stove and its contents. "Will your French creation ooze with Camembert and fresh lavender?"

"I can't afford Camembert." Her lips curved easily as she headed for the cheese board. "Swiss cheese was only two dollars a pound this week, and I asked the woman at the deli to slice the cheese extra thin."

"Did she oblige?"

"Indeed." Belle returned to the stove and glanced at him over her shoulder. "The clerks recognize me. For your information, coupons and specials can result in substantial grocery savings."

He savored another sip of the refreshing tea, allowing the flavors of sweet and sour to linger on his tongue. "Is this a fact?"

"From first-hand experience."

He gave an overstated groan. "Are you one of those customers who hold up the entire grocery line so that the clerk can scan your fifty cent coupon?"

"That's me."

She was so serious he chuckled. His ex-wife had never clipped a coupon in her life.

For several minutes he sat silently, allowing his luncheon hostess an opportunity to prepare the omelet, correction *omelette*, without interruption.

He used the minutes to contemplate the next phase of his firm's expansion, but soon chose to reflect on his surprising good fortune.

Belle Boots stood five feet away from him at her shiny, stainless steel stove.

And he liked that—being with her, sharing lunch.

During the never-ending evenings he'd spent alone since his divorce—he'd never envisioned himself living in any other manner other than as a single man. Absorbed in his business and raising his daughter, he'd convinced himself that he was better off alone.

For starters, just look what he'd accomplished since his divorce. Why, his firm had doubled in size. Imagine if he had a demanding wife to please, as during the seven years of marriage to Rowena.

Therefore, he'd be happier if he remained unattached, apart from an occasional, impersonal date. Any free time was earmarked for his precious daughter.

After weeks of texting and phoning Belle, he was inclined

to remain on the same course. Belle had encouraged him to examine aspects of life he'd overlooked—the outdoors, nature, and humorous banter—and that made him uncomfortable. However, not so uncomfortable he'd give up his frenetic work pace.

Besides, by Sunday evening he'd be on the road again, continuing his commitment to excellent design over cheap construction, connecting with Megan through Skype, while reassured that the nanny provided excellent care.

He and his firm fought for projects to be completed without politics interfering. That was all well and good, but left little time for laughing conversations with Belle, or water fights with a hose, or heartfelt discussions concerning his daughter.

Or, he amended with a smile, any fainting goats.

Whenever he mentioned Megan, compassion and concern would immediately touch Belle's features.

As he lifted his glass, Belle flipped the omelette as adeptly as any French chef. She shook the pan constantly over the gas stove's flame.

When she slanted him a glance, he made a show of applause. She flamboyantly bowed, then turned back to the stove to flick dashes of black pepper and basil on the eggs.

His heart skipped a beat at her exuberance, her enthusiasm. He sat back, indulging himself by staring at her slim profile and exquisite features. She was a natural beauty.

What if he'd met her soon after his divorce? Would she have been able to teach him how to forgive, to assuage his jaded heart? Would she have encouraged him to seek ambitions more gratifying than wealth and influence and acknowledgment—motivations that had molded his childhood and adulthood? He was, after all, a Bransfield, and well aware of his illustrious legacy.

The improbability of ever meeting Belle when he was at an earlier age surfaced, and he checked himself. At what cocktail party would they have connected? His life had revolved around affluence before his father had lost everything because of laziness and indifference. To be successful, a business required continuous monitoring and long business hours.

Sure, monetary and societal advantages had been a given in Scotland, and Andrew and his sister's seats among the elite were secured.

During those years, an equine therapist named Belle would never have entered his sphere of aristocratic friends.

Even if they'd met, would he have been interested? More than likely not, for she would have been overshadowed by the fashionable and ostentatious women. Belle wouldn't have been comfortable if he had escorted her to an exclusive country club dinner.

Or would she? No doubt, she was as gorgeous in a fancy ball gown as in jeans.

Distractedly, he envisioned her in an elegant green silk, her dark hair combed to the side and secured with a glittering diamond pin.

He rolled his glass between his palms, striving to be completely truthful with himself while Belle focused on her skillet creation.

When he was younger, he would have respected her intelligence and openness, her kind-heartedness, her pure, fresh nature.

But he wouldn't have asked her out.

However, that was then. This was now.

"Watch, Andrew." Belle signaled him over as she tilted the pan, added a generous sprinkling of cheese and slid it onto a plate. "This is what makes a French omelette different from an American-style. It's all in the rolling. See? The omelette is in the shape of an oval, whereas an American omelet is folded in half."

"Thus, you produced a perfect omelet," he said.

"*Omelette.*" She held up the plate. "Voila!"

Laughing, he pressed a kiss on her forehead.

He couldn't help himself. She was a woman who needed to be appreciated and kissed.

"Belle Boots, you are priceless." He chucked her beneath her chin. "Thank you for helping me to laugh again."

"It's good to laugh, isn't it?"

Her assertion called for another kiss. "I haven't enjoyed myself this much in eons."

"Eons?"

"Months … years."

"I haven't laughed this much in eons, either." She reached for napkins, plates, and forks, then arranged two settings on the kitchen island.

"Did you study cooking in college?" He waited for her to sit before taking his place across from her.

She shrugged and looked away. "Most of my college courses were related to equine therapy.

"Is that a bad thing? Equine therapy?"

"Not at all."

"What courses did you study?"

"I earned an undergraduate degree in counseling. Afterward, I completed a certification program, focusing on equine interaction."

"Which is?"

"To treat patients, particularly children, with emotional or physical disabilities through a mutual affection for horses."

"You're obviously passionate about your work."

"I am. Except …" She grimaced and shifted in her seat.

"Except?"

"Except my parents expected me to become a doctor like my father. I might have satisfied them if I had pursued a veterinarian degree." Belle sighed. "I considered it ..."

"And then?"

"I love animals but also aspired to help people. My major seemed a suitable way to incorporate both."

"Did you? Please your parents?" he asked.

"No. They tried to steer my aspirations to match theirs. Obviously they didn't succeed." A sheen of tears shimmered in her velvety gray eyes, and she concentrated on a circle of copper pots hanging from the ceiling.

"Embrace your profession." He grabbed her hand. "You're improving lives and helping your students overcome emotional and physical trauma."

"Am I? Truly?"

"I speak from experience because you changed Megan's life." Reassuringly, he squeezed her fingers. "Most definitely."

She kept her focus on the pots. "Or maybe I studied equine therapy to become something my parents didn't want me to be."

Had she suppressed those contemplations, or silently contemplated them all these years? She'd spoken quickly, then seemed to regret her outburst.

"We are all rebellious once in a while," he said. "I was certainly unmanageable when I first moved to America."

"Why?"

"Because going from affluence to poverty, especially in an unfamiliar country, was disheartening." Andrew rubbed his forehead. "My mother never forgave my father for his poor business decisions."

"And you?"

"I did my own thing, made my own way."

"Your sister?"

"In Kate's opinion, my father could do no wrong." He drew a long breath and curled his fingers around hers. "Tell me something, Belle. Are you content?"

"Undeniably."

"Then stay true to who you are and be happy with your choice. My grandfather in Scotland used to say, "You're a long time deid.'"

"Dead? That goes without saying?"

"Once you're dead, you're dead for a long time, so enjoy life."

"Not the most heartening of Scottish sayings," she muttered.

"But true, nonetheless."

The thought flitted through his mind that he should take the saying to heart. He was committed to a continuous strive for perfection and success, pushing too fast on a narrow lane, but he couldn't help himself.

He remembered what it was like to lose everything.

Never again.

Belle eyed their plates. "Our food is getting cold."

"We can't let your creation go to waste. I'm impressed by your expertise."

"I watch numerous demonstrations on television, and you can learn a lot from YouTube."

"I'm sure, and we mustn't waste all those eggs."

She bowed her head and said grace, something Andrew had never done, although his demeanor was suitably prayerful. When she finished, he forked a mouthful of omelette and closed his eyes, savoring the delectable combination of finely cooked eggs combined with the velvety smoothness of milky sweet cheese.

"Pure dead brilliant," he said, and Belle smiled at the compliment.

He washed down the omelette with another glass of iced tea.

After lunch was over, he helped her clear and rinse the plates.

When the kitchen was tidied to her satisfaction, she brewed a pot of coffee and arranged a set of glass mugs on the island.

Over steaming coffee, he said, "Again, I'm sorry the goats fainted. My habit is to shut the door with my foot because I usually carry papers or tools—"

"No explanation is necessary, Andrew." Lightly, she touched his hand. "The goats are healthy, and actually, they didn't faint. Myotonic goats just stiffen and fall over, appearing to faint."

"I felt like I should rush over to splash cold water on their faces to revive them." He hadn't, because he didn't care to be near two stiff goats, especially one as ornery looking as Hester. "But they were up again in a few seconds and didn't seem hurt."

Belle's eyes sparkled. "No negative consequences."

A radiant sun lit the kitchen, and tiny silver hoops glinted from her ears.

Beyond the expansive window over the sink, vibrant purple zinnias blossomed beneath carefully trimmed hedging and a white oak tree. Belle had mentioned that Abby and Felix were avid gardeners.

Belle smoothed the napkin on her lap. Her movements were elegant, and he admired her aura of kindness. Despite the hard manual exertion in the stalls, her fingers were long and slender and diligently clean. Poignantly, he recalled her adjusting Megan's horse helmet, ensuring that his daughter was safe and protected.

"To put your mind at ease," she continued, "fainting doesn't hurt a goat nor cause any pain."

He gazed at her and smiled. He couldn't get enough of seeing her, being with her. She was naturally sophisticated, humorous, and captivating. She'd been forced to move from Roses quickly, and the sadness she felt at leaving her precious students was real. Despite her optimism, the move hadn't been easy.

And the attention she showed her animals was diligent and caring.

He was a decade older, and a hundred times more world-weary. Yet, every minute with her put another chink in his inflexible armor toward life.

Where Belle was concerned, things weren't all business, and her empathy softened him.

"I leave on Sunday to work in Roses for a couple days. Adella will care for Megan." He glanced at his watch. They were scheduled to return to the house so Megan could take her afternoon nap.

"If you see Candee in Roses, tell her how much I miss her and her family," Belle replied. "With the blur of moving, I haven't had time to phone, except for a quick text to refer Joseph to another therapist."

"How is he doing?"

"The therapist is excellent, although I miss Joseph."

"I'm sure he misses you too." Andrew pushed back his stool. Belle did the same. "I'll return to Wilmington by midweek. Thank you for a delicious lunch."

She walked him to the entryway. "Thank *you* for the gorgeous flowers."

"My pleasure. I'm a romantic at heart.

He was? Well, with Belle he was becoming a regular Romeo.

"You're a sensitive and kind man."

"And princely?"

"Sure."

"And you're a wonderful woman. A princess." More than

wonderful. More than a princess. That prickle of awareness whenever she was near flooded his senses.

Out of the corner of his eye he spotted an orange tabby. The cat shot from the hallway and skirted around his legs before disappearing.

"Ginger," Belle supplied.

"Ginger. Right. Okay. Will Ginger bite?"

"Not that I'm aware."

"Does Ginger have a sister or brother?"

Belle elbowed him. "No."

"I'm starting to think you live in a glorified petting zoo."

She burst out laughing. "Don't tell me you're going to make a scene whenever you see one of my animals?"

"Never." He tugged her close. "But I'll show you what a scene looks like."

He didn't give her time to catch her breath nor fire a snappy rejoinder, because he kissed her, long and deep.

"That's quite a scene," she murmured between his kisses. "An extremely romantic one."

"It's from a Scottish movie."

"Which is?"

"Braveheart."

"You mean the movie with the stunning camera work?"

"The very same." He nuzzled her neck. "I'll text you while I'm gone. Will you miss me?"

She pulled back and brushed stray blades of dried grass from his shirt, giving him a tender look with those gorgeous gray eyes. "I'm a pushover for a man who shows up at my riding ring bearing flowers. Especially flowers he snagged at a great sale." She granted him one of her heart-stopping smiles.

Thus, she offered all the proof he needed. He kissed her again and would have continued. Unfortunately, his cellphone chirped, jerking him back to reality.

He snatched the phone from his pocket while muttering a string of colorful Scottish phrases. As Belle stepped away, he scanned the text message from his foreman.

Problem with a work site in Camden, SC, boss.

Which site? Andrew texted.

The healthcare renovation at the senior living facility. Construction debris containment, and an extremely vocal town board who are concerned about infection control. They're demanding a meeting with you at eight a.m. on Monday morning or they're shutting the project down.

He pushed out a sigh.

"Troubles with Megan?" Belle asked.

"Thankfully, Megan is fine. An addition to an existing building I've designed is more complex than anticipated, and the board insists the healthcare facility remain in operation while the addition is completed."

"Is it possible to keep the facility open?"

"Not easily, but necessary because the logistics of moving senior citizens to another facility would be difficult." He shoved a hand through his hair. "Part of the problem is economics. The city paid for the renovation. The crew isn't as fastidious about debris as they should be, which leads to a cleanliness issue. The town requires a meeting with me or construction ceases."

"Is a solution possible?"

He slipped on his boots. "Anything is possible."

He insisted on a standard of excellence, not adapting lightly to changes. He thrust his cellphone into his pocket after replying to his foreman. *I'll arrive in Camden by Sunday afternoon so we can talk this over before the Monday meeting.*

This issue would push back his trip to Roses, and consequently, his return to Wilmington.

And this newest demand reminded him that what had happened in Belle's apartment would never happen again.

His work was a part of himself he wouldn't relinquish. Through his designs, his visions became realities.

In truth, being recognized by pleased customers motivated him. Consequently, he would carry out whatever orders were enforced in order to satisfy the requirements for the Camden, SC, town board.

CHAPTER 6

Summer visitors flooded Wilmington, and the intense heat of a southern July eased on.

Belle began offering equine therapy sessions and hadn't seen Andrew since he'd departed for Camden. His texts to her were short and concise.

The first arrived on Sunday.

Hi Belle. I'm in Camden. Here is Adella's cellphone number. Store it in your contacts and text her directly regarding Megan's sessions.

In other words, no communication with him.

Will do. And your drive to Camden was ...? Belle texted.

She grimaced. She'd never been good at texting. She was literally all thumbs.

Uneventful, came his reply. *What did you do this weekend?*

I was busy. Still unpacking. Plus, I visited my Aunt Lucinda.

Her aunt had remarked that she was pleased Belle had begun a new chapter in her life, grinning when Belle mentioned Andrew numerous times. With each recounting of the services he provided, Aunt Lucinda had stretched her hand across the porch swing to pat Belle's arm. "You found someone special. Don't throw love away, like I did."

"Didn't you once say men were a bother?"

"A woman has the prerogative to change her mind and admit her mistakes. If the right man comes along—"

"Andrew and I aren't serious," Belle had protested.

"You will be."

Belle had a swift, unbidden thought that Aunt Lucinda might be correct.

With a sigh, she batted away the contemplation. Sure, she felt special when she was with him, and they chatted about everything because he was easy to talk to. But she'd given her heart to someone only to have her dreams broken.

How is your aunt? Andrew texted.

Eccentric, as usual. She insisted on wearing green gloves and an Indiana Jones hat when we shopped at the Farmer's Market.

Did anyone remark on her appearance?

After all these years, they're accustomed to her.

Does she use coupons too? he asked.

LOL, no. What about you?

No coupons.

I mean, how was your weekend?

More unpacking, same as you. Spent hours with Megan before I drove to Camden. Look, I gotta go. My foreman is pounding on my hotel door.

Good luck with the meeting.

Thanks. Hope your week goes well.

You too.

Impersonal, affable, informal. Hurried. No mention of their lunch together. No mention of French omelettes or tabby cats. This wasn't the teasing, good-natured man who had kissed her by the fence, or in the entryway of her apartment.

This was a different Andrew. The entrepreneur. The billionaire. The man firmly out of reach.

When her cellphone pinged the following week, her heart stopped when his name crossed her screen.

Crazy busy here, Andrew texted. *How are you?*

Fine. You?

Overloaded in work.

The project is taking longer than anticipated?

Much longer.

She waited for him to continue. When he didn't, she asked, *Are you there?*

Sorry, Belle. I'm preoccupied. A local crew was hired, and it's up to me to maintain a high benchmark. Safety is our first priority.

Lots of details?

Yes. I've divided off part of the construction with barriers and stay on site to ensure the crew is complying with town regulations.

Numerous problems waiting for only you to solve?

Okay, that was edgy, but it was too late to take it back. Another long hesitation, and she watched her phone screen for the telltale bubbles indicating that he was texting.

Architects like solving problems, Belle. BTW, Megan is loving her sessions with you.

She's a pleasure. Belle's fingers hovered over her phone's keyboard. Should she inquire when he planned on returning to Wilmington? She typed the question, quickly deleting it. Too needy.

Take care of yourself, she typed in its place. *Don't work too hard.* Ugh. Such a cliché. She pulled at the collar of her sleeveless denim shirt.

That's my job, Belle.

That's your life, she wanted to fire back. Instead, she said nothing.

. . .

SEVERAL DAYS AFTERWARD, she claimed a stool at her kitchen island and examined the bouquet of dahlias—the petals brown and curling, the stalks drooping.

Nonetheless, a slight yellow tint remained. A sign of hope.

She re-cut the stems, changed the old water to fresh and returned them to the vase.

What is the meaning of yellow flowers? she typed into her cellphone.

Daisies mean cheerfulness and innocence. Dahlias represent a forever commitment between two persons.

She sucked in a breath. She couldn't focus on any words with tears flooding her eyes.

"I looked up the meanings of the flowers," Andrew had told her. *"Dahlias seemed more appropriate."*

Slowly, her annoyance at him for being preoccupied in Camden gave way to regret that he wasn't with her in Wilmington. Unfortunately, her practical brain reminded, that same romantic man had forgotten all about her only in a matter of days.

ON A LEISURELY WALK A WEEK LATER, Belle came upon a street sign that read Carolina Way. Andrew was in Camden, she rationalized, and she was more than a little curious to see his house. Besides, she enjoyed viewing real estate, assuming that someday she'd have a home of her own.

As she strolled the shore, she relished the slap of ocean water against the rocks, the Atlantic-blue churning surf. All familiar. All soothing. She loved living in Wilmington again.

She neared a secluded mansion and verified the location using the map on her cellphone. One Carolina Way. Andrew's house.

Her lips parted. She stood silent in mute confusion.

His "little" place? Painted a vivid turquoise blue, the spectacular home sat directly on the ocean and claimed a broad, sandy beach.

This was his rental—with the outsized swimming pool flanked by elegant Roman columns, complemented by faultlessly groomed shrubs? Really?

Yes, really, because, clutching a cellphone, he waved to her from the second-floor balcony.

Her legs froze in place. Wasn't he supposed to be in Camden? He'd caught her spying on him.

At any rate, he'd returned and had obviously neglected to phone her.

And what was it with this man and balconies?

Despite her compulsion to flee, she gathered her courage and feigned a smile. "Hi." She enhanced her smile with a high-spirited wave. "I took a walk and—" *Happened to be strolling along Carolina Way? Why were her thoughts so muddled?* "This is private property, correct?"

He clicked off his cellphone. "It's *my* private property, Belle, and you're always welcome. Adella just left, and Megan is in bed."

Belle's hands curled. "I assumed you were out of town." Okay, she was incriminating herself further. Not to mention that she was shouting and had no right to question his whereabouts.

"The problems in Camden are resolved, and I arrived home an hour ago. I showered and read Megan a story before her bedtime. I planned to phone you when I finished this last business call and here you are. C'mon over." He waved her forward.

"I can't." She peered at her cut-off shorts. Her hair must look a sight, and sand had taken up permanent residence in her sandals. "Thanks for the invite, but I'll take a raincheck." She hastened her steps and backed away from the house.

"Belle, please. I'll meet you on the deck." That Scottish lilt, affirming an unpretentious warmth, both enchanting and entrancing. He slid his cellphone into the pocket of his gray polo shirt. "We can watch the sunset together."

Ever the romantic.

She swallowed her protest, slowly starting up the lush expanse of emerald lawn. He was sensitive and seemed sincere, she conceded, and the combination was irresistible.

As she approached, she took in the inviting scene. Candles were lit on a teak credenza, and a Mozart piano sonata played from an invisible speaker. The dancing flames from a rectangular fire pit beckoned, and potted red zinnias brought radiant color to the deck.

He finished arranging two white Adirondack chairs on either side of a wooden table, set a child monitor nearby, then surveyed Belle from head to toe. Striding forward, he grasped her hands in his. "Miss Belle Boots, you are adorable."

"Adorable?"

"You always remind me of a poster woman for ... I don't know ... small-town goodness."

"Is that a Scottish compliment?"

"American." He laughed. "In any event, you're gorgeous and a perfect package."

Promptly recognizing that after two weeks on the road, any woman would undoubtedly be a perfect package, she took a guarded step backward.

"How are you?" A Scottish burr laced his words, trilling the 'r.'

"I'm fine. You?" She gazed up at his impossibly attractive face. Would he welcome her into his arms?

He didn't, murmuring he was also fine and gesturing for her to sit. "Can I offer you anything to drink?" he asked. "You name it, I have it."

"Iced tea."

"Ah, sweet iced tea. My beverage of choice is non-alcoholic Scottish ginger beer this evening. Adella picked up a six-pack at a local specialty store. Are you up to trying it?"

"Sure. Was the beer on sale?"

"We're just glad the store carries it." He grabbed two bottles from a free-standing mini fridge tucked in the corner of the deck. "Adella would have paid any price, especially because it's on my tab." He grinned and Belle reciprocated.

He gazed at her as he poured beer into her glass. "You are lovely."

"A minute ago, your choice phrases were adorable and small-town goodness."

"Pure dead brilliant also comes to mind and beautiful and I—" His words rushed together. "Sorry. Scots don't give praise well."

She studied the glass as he continued pouring. "You're spilling the beer," she noted.

He muttered a lively Gaelic phrase, reached for a linen napkin to mop the overflow, then handed her an overflowing glass.

She sniffed, then tasted, rewarded with a sampling of spicy ginger and citrus.

He set the bottle upright and waited for her to sit, then claimed the chair beside hers. "Good?"

She lifted her glass. "Delicious."

Judging from his reddish beard stubble, he hadn't shaved in several days. His hair was still damp from the shower and his shirt, open at the throat, was tucked into olive-colored shorts. Involuntarily, she memorized the way he looked, the rigid planes of his chest, the strong profile—every inch the charismatic male. She also noted the fixed lines of fatigue around his eyes and mouth, which she hadn't noticed when she'd last seen him.

He smiled and leaned back. "Do I meet with your approval?"

"Sorry. I was staring, wasn't I?"

"Don't be sorry. You meet with my approval too." There was no mistaking his quiet assertion. Despite his laid-back teasing, her pulse doubled.

She shifted. Swallowed. Even if she had the courage to ask him why he'd texted her only twice, she couldn't be certain whether her question wouldn't come with an answer she wasn't prepared to hear.

"Thanks for repairing my leaky roof," she said. "Abby and Felix gratefully appreciated your generosity."

"My pleasure." Andrew stretched out his long legs, picked up his glass and watched the fire's cheery blaze leaping and flickering. "I, too, fix things, except my specialty is buildings."

She sat straighter. "You remember I'm a fixer?"

"There's nothing about you I ever forget." A warmhearted gleam shone from his eyes. "Did Candee mention I visited her when I was in Roses?"

Belle placed her glass aside. "Briefly, yes."

"Did she say who we discussed?"

Recalling their phone conversation, Belle replied in a cool voice, "She was evasive." And that had made Belle uncomfortable. "I assume you two discussed Joseph's new horse therapist, or Megan, or Bransfield Designs." Noting the rigidity in his jaw, Belle ended with a short laugh. "Correct?"

ANDREW SET down his glass and reached for Belle, although she drew away and planted her hands on her lap. Despite her off-the-cuff response, he had the uneasy impression he'd unintentionally upset her. Determining their conversation required a clearer explanation, he began, "Candee and I discussed you."

"Me?" Belle tilted her head. "Why?"

"I was eager to learn more about you. After considerable prodding, Candee was kind enough to share the details of your marriage with me."

"You mean my divorce?"

"From what I understand, you were married to a guy named Tyler who didn't appreciate you."

Slender eyebrows snapped together. "Why were you two discussing my personal life?"

He caught the resentment lacing her tone. "I explained why. I'm interested in you, Belle. Surely you realize that."

Well, that wasn't the entire truth. He was *more* than interested.

In Camden, he hadn't been able to think clearly, which had put him in a state he wasn't accustomed to, causing the job to take twice as long. He'd been certain when he'd left Wilmington that a relationship with Belle was too emotionally harrowing to contemplate. However, sitting next to her now played havoc with his sentiments.

She kept her gaze on the ocean. Her fingers toyed with the silky hair at her temple.

"Look at me." He touched his lips to her restless fingers. "Talk to me."

"About my failed marriage? About Tyler?"

"If you wish."

"Hasn't Candee regaled you with all the tragic, pathetic details?"

"They're not pathetic," he said. "And I'd like to hear them from you."

Her gaze darted to his. "We're friends, aren't we?"

"Without question."

"Alright then." She plucked up her glass. "To begin with, Tyler was in my life for several years. I believed I loved him."

Despite the irrationality of it, a surge of jealousy went through Andrew.

The air became unnaturally quiet.

"When I first met him, he asked if I could keep a secret. He'd been hurt by several unpleasant relationships and had lost faith in women. I felt bad for him and privileged that he confided in me. He was such a stoic man. He was a professional accountant, you know."

Andrew gave a bitter laugh. "I heard."

"A string of unfortunate luck, Tyler told me." Belle's heel incessantly tapped on the wooden deck. "His sad stories inspired me to prove to him that he shouldn't lose faith in women and love."

"Did you succeed?"

Belle choked on her beer. "A month after we were married he verbally degraded me after a horse competition, mocking that I smelled like a barn."

The sadness, the humiliation brimming from her gray eyes, drew a dawning of compassion within him. That frozen ocean of deep uncertainty—to care for a woman again—to care for anyone save his precious daughter; began to crack.

He laid a palm on Belle's cheek. He longed to embrace her, to hold on to the intense emotions gripping him, the first real emotions he'd felt in years. He wanted to share more than a moment with her. He anticipated sharing a lifetime.

The knowledge surprised him, but only for an instant. He embraced it for what it was. The truth.

A tear ran down her face and he kissed her there, sampling the saltiness. He rifled through his intentions to continue the conversation, half-heartedly rejecting the subject of her beauty, her mesmerizing smile, her declaration that they were friends.

They were more than friends. Much more.

"Go on," he said tenderly.

She fixed her glass on the table. "Six months into our marriage, Tyler screamed at me for not keeping myself up to his excessive standards. He scolded me for always wearing informal clothes." She bit down on her bottom lip as it quivered. "I tried to reason with him. Jeans were, after all, what a therapist wore when around horses all day. But he merely yelled louder. His profession required a well-dressed woman he could escort to corporate dinners." She gazed up at Andrew with tear-filled eyes. "I didn't provide a proper fit for him."

Andrew kept his features neutral, although his insides churned with fury. "Your beauty rivals any of the prettiest starlets."

"I'm adorable, if I remember your words correctly."

"And lovely," he emphasized.

She waved an airy hand, dismissing his compliments. "The next day Tyler apologized for his outburst. Nonetheless, a few days afterward he filed for divorce. He told me I couldn't compare to his glamorous ex-girlfriends if I tried."

"He told you he'd dated glamorous women?"

Her chin lowered. "Often."

Andrew recalled Belle's hands gently fastening Megan's helmet, her soothing, encouraging voice, their shared giggles when his daughter rode Honeycrisp.

He marveled at her kindness, suppressing a frown because now she was assiduously avoiding his stare. For all her dauntless independence, wit, and spirit, she became hesitant and withdrawn when talking about Tyler.

"The papers from his lawyer decreed irreconcilable differences," Belle was saying.

"You should have been glad to get rid of him." Andrew evened out his voice, seeking to reassure her while tamping down the impulse to physically strangle her ex.

"My aunt said the same. So did Candee. I should've known by the way Jenkins reacted the first time Tyler entered his stall."

"Your horse, you mean?"

"Yes, I believe animals have a sixth sense." Briefly, Belle closed her eyes. "I keenly remember Jenkins' soft brown eyes going hard, and his ears pinned back. That marked the last time Tyler ever entered his stall."

"Tyler never tried again?"

"Once, but Jenkins threatened to kick him."

"So Tyler got the memo?"

"Loud and clear." She grinned, but her expression swiftly turned sober. "But you know what?" She picked up her glass. Her hand shook. "When the divorce documents arrived, I accepted and signed while my heart broke."

"Why? You clearly were abused."

"In my mind I was a failure—trying to fix Tyler, trying to fix my marriage, and ultimately not gratifying my parents' wishes."

"You chose to follow your own professional path, and for that I commend you." Andrew raised his glass for a toast.

She clinked her glass against his. "True."

They exchanged congratulatory glances.

Her thick hair gleamed in the firelight, spilling forward across her face. Her lashes, dark and lush, cast the hint of a shadow across her unblemished cheeks.

"I'm wondering if you ever really loved Tyler." Andrew voiced his thoughts aloud. Although perhaps he shouldn't have because her eyebrows pulled together and she frowned.

"Maybe. Maybe not." She stood, and he admired her pure loveliness, the subtle finesse in the way she wore her clothes, no matter how casual.

She peered at the sun setting on the horizon, the sky a brilliant brush of vivid rose and intense orange, the waves shimmering like diamonds as an unflinching moon cast silvery beams on the water.

He came behind her and enfolded her in his arms, tracing the curve of her ear with his mouth. She trembled. He hoped she would turn to gaze at him so he could see her face.

When she didn't turn, he brushed his knuckles against her cheek and delicately kissed her shoulders, her nape, her hair.

"Andrew, I—"

"Don't, Belle."

"Don't what?"

He drew in a slow, leaden breath. "Don't ever change."

Because he was falling in love with her.

She brought him a quiet sense of joy. In quick-thinking texts, emotional moments, and dazzling smiles, she'd stolen his heart.

His words wrung a hesitant chuckle from her. "Don't ever change what? My profession?"

"Anything about you."

"Are you saying that you're beginning to like horses?"

"Fortunately, you're not a horse."

"I'm around them all week."

He smirked. "I'll manage."

"You haven't met Jenkins face to face yet." She threw a rueful smile over her shoulder, and he set his sights on her alluring lips.

He laughed, deep and throaty, steadying himself, marveling at her bewitching effect on him. Impulsively, he tightened his arms around her. He couldn't get enough of her, and this was a unique experience. Yes, women had been a social duty all his adult life, but certainly not his entire world. He'd never been preoccupied with a woman before.

"Andrew?"

He closed his eyes. "Hmm?"

"Are you interested in hearing the rest of my story?"

Even with his eyes closed, he felt her gaze on him as she turned and rested her soft cheek against his chest.

The simple affection of her movements plunged his spirits. Effectively, it reminded him that if he stopped seeing her, there would be no further tender moments.

He should let her go. He was committed to his work, to his daughter. There was no room in his life for another relationship. Another failure.

Not in business. Not personally. He'd learned that hard lesson from experience.

But he *couldn't* let Belle go.

"Yes. Tell me everything." He opened his eyes. "Under one condition."

"What's that?"

Huskily, he murmured, "I can keep my arms around you."

For a beat she was silent, followed by a quiet sigh.

"I'd love that," she whispered.

He tipped up her head, prompting her with an over bright smile. "I'm listening."

"Right …well … " She inhaled. "When I rationalized my situation, I attributed my divorce to a marriage gone wrong at an early age and a manipulative husband. I shouldn't have tried to fix his problems."

"Fixers place other people's needs before their own," Andrew said.

"I have an overwhelming urge to support folks, and try to come up with a solution to make things better. Sometimes, I can't help myself."

"Sometimes?"

"Oftentimes," she conceded.

Her eyes reminded him of the color of dove feathers, soft and gentle, which perfectly described his selfless, caring Belle.

The last beams of sunlight streamed down, enhancing her shiny hair with golden highlights.

She interrupted his delightful contemplation by rhapsodizing, "Isn't the sky picturesque? The sun sets over the ocean in so many colors. It resembles a portrait."

"Or a painting on canvas." He cradled her close to his chest. "Sometimes I forget to appreciate the precious things in life."

Like love.

He'd never known what love felt like. Now he did.

The exhilaration, the joy. The feeling that every last breath had been taken from his lungs.

Love wasn't planned. It never was.

And love was the only thing in life that truly mattered.

CHAPTER 7

*T*he night Belle had watched the sunset with Andrew, she'd agreed to text him the minute she returned to her apartment. Touched and flattered when he'd insisted, she'd happily obliged.

Twenty-four hours later, he suggested dinner with him and Megan when he came back to Wilmington the following weekend.

She accepted.

He canceled soon afterward. Problems in Camden.

The days merged into another week before he arrived back in Wilmington.

When can I see you again? he texted. *My foreman told me there are wild horses on a beach in the Outer Banks.*

You mean in Corolla? she asked.

Yes.

Megan will love this, Belle replied.

I missed you while I was away.

Audibly, she swallowed, processing Andrew's comment.

And you? he pressed. *You love horses.*

A given. But he'd been gone. Now he assumed she was at his beck and call.

Wild horses will be a grand adventure, she hedged.

I agree. BTW, Megan's eye patch was removed this week.

I know. I saw her when she came for her session. How wonderful.

I wasn't around. I relied on Adella to bring Megan for her eyeglass fitting, because work necessitated that I stay in Camden. Still, I should have been there.

I would have enthusiastically joined them, Belle responded.

Really?

Without question. I love Megan.

Thank you. A hesitation filled the space between them. *That means a lot.*

Wait …The horses at the Outer Banks wander freely, Belle texted. *What if a horse gallops near you?*

I'd jump into the ocean.

She laughed out loud. *Sounds like a plan.*

Not a particularly good plan, but a plan, nonetheless.

Are you aware Corolla is four hours away from Wilmington by car? she added.

It is?

Aren't you aware of the distance?

I've been so preoccupied lately.

Perhaps a beach trip somewhere a bit closer?

I missed you, he texted a second time. *Will you come to the beach with us?*

She squeezed her cellphone, briefly closing her eyes while her heartbeat soared.

"You missed me," she whispered to the phone screen, visualizing his handsome face.

She'd missed him too, but she wouldn't tell him that.

You work too much, she typed instead.

No, no, too bossy.

She deleted it. He'd just arrived after several nonstop workdays.

I'm trying to change, he texted, as if he had read her mind. *I tuned in to a bunch of self-help audiobooks during the long drive. How to balance work with everyday life.*

Were the books helpful?

Interesting. Thought-provoking.

Perhaps he should practice what he listened to.

Still, a much-needed beach respite would allow Andrew a renewed and refreshed outlook.

Don't mention anything else on this subject, she warned herself before her fingers touched the keypad. She had no right trying to fix him.

Shall I pack a lunch? she inquired.

No. You have enough to do. There's a certain colonel who makes a delicious fried chicken.

I thought you loved fresh seafood?

Who said that? Me?

Uh, huh. Fresh caught fish for dinner…

Hmm. We'll order seafood when we get closer to the beach. Pan-fried scallops and fried pickles are my favorite. Megan likes chicken strips.

Scallops sound good. Undecided on the pickles. Which beach?

The beach in front of my house.

You just went from a four-hour car ride to a one minute car ride. Have you considered Carolina Beach?

Is it far?

About twenty minutes away.

She loved the sun-drenched feel of the modest town and hadn't had the opportunity to visit since landing in Wilmington.

Excellent. I'll pick you up at ten on Saturday morning.

. . .

TWO DAYS LATER, Andrew and Megan arrived at Belle's apartment exactly as her cuckoo clock chimed ten a.m. Punctuality was a trait Belle admired about him.

What did it cost him to juggle a multi-million-dollar business while single parenting? Sure, he had the means and domestic help, but it still required resourcefulness and a perseverance she seldom witnessed in men. Certainly not Tyler. Certainly not any she'd dated since her divorce.

Of course, she and Andrew weren't dating. They were friends who shared a common interest in his daughter's happiness and security.

And horses.

Well, not horses, exactly. Goats. Nope. Tabby cats. Umm, no.

Nonetheless, they got along splendidly.

AS WAS HIS CUSTOM, Andrew got out of his SUV as soon as Belle emerged from her apartment.

He opened the passenger door for her. "You are stunning," he said.

"Thank you, but hardly." She glanced down at the khaki shorts and red ribbed tank top she'd worn over her swimsuit. "I appreciate your earlier home-town goodness compliment, though."

"Small-town goodness," he corrected. "Here's another compliment. 'A pretty face suits the dish-cloth.'"

"Now I look like a dish-cloth?" She hung her hands on her hips. "Is that a step up or down from small-town goodness?"

"It's Scottish flattery. You are stunning in anything you wear." He chucked her under the chin. "So it's a step up."

"Well, perhaps if you said it in Scottish …"

"English will do." He grabbed her raffia bag and feigned a groan as he fixed it in the trunk. "What's in this? Lead?"

"All the necessary supplies. Sunscreen, towels, water bottles and my script." Belle displayed a tablet from her tote bag, settled into the SUV's plush leather upholstery and greeted Megan with a jovial smile.

The child sat securely buckled in her car seat. Her emerald-colored eyes, enhanced by raspberry eyeglass frames, twinkled with excitement.

"Hi, Miss Belle." Megan lifted her terry cloth cover-up with exaggerated flair. "Do you like my bathing suit?"

"I love pink unicorns," Belle replied. "And you are utterly adorable."

"Daddy helped dress me, but I picked out my own clothes."

"Kudos to you and daddy." Belle grinned as Andrew winked at her.

"A script, Belle?" He slipped into the driver's seat. "As in a movie script?"

"Not quite Hollywood, I'm afraid, but yes."

"You act as well as offer equine therapy? I'm impressed."

"Thanks. The Little Theater in Wilmington put out a casting call for The Lion, The Witch, and The Wardrobe." She glanced at her tablet before embarking on details.

"C.S. Lewis?"

"Very good."

"Daddy, you read that story to me," Megan said. "I like the part when the four kids go into the wardrobe and all the animals talk."

"Their world is magical." Belle grinned at Megan over her shoulder, then gazed ahead. "The story's message focuses on faith and courage."

"Don't forget love," Andrew said. For a split-second he

watched her, the heat in his tone igniting his words. "Because in the end, it's all about love."

His deep voice, that Scottish brogue, his green, fathomless eyes, had an alarming effect on Belle's heart rate. The remark was so typical of his romantic nature that she smiled.

"Is it?" she asked.

"What the world needs now … All you need is … you've heard the lyrics to these popular songs, correct?"

"Of course."

"I wasn't certain, because you're younger than me."

"By only a few years." She rolled her eyes in amused exasperation. "You're certainly brimming with all sorts of sayings this morning."

He wore a pair of swim trunks in a dashing pattern of tropical leaves, and a royal-blue T-shirt that read *Bransfield Designs*. He was drop-dead handsome, and his debonair attitude mesmerized her. Another Andrew she was beginning to know better—this one playful and humorous.

When he rolled down the windows, a breeze grabbed her hair. Deeply, she breathed in, delighting in the scents of fish and salt, the promise of the ocean.

He switched on the radio to a station with kid-safe lyrics and transferred it to the back speakers. Immediately, Megan and Belle hummed along to a familiar tune.

"Belle, are you auditioning for the role of Mrs. Beaver?" Andrew asked.

"Mr. Beaver's wife?" Belle stopped humming, glancing at him as he concentrated on the road. "The obsessive, overly careful woman?"

"If I remember correctly, Mrs. Beaver is kind-hearted."

"I'll need to audition first before I'm cast in one of the bigger roles. Fortunately, there's always a place in the supporting cast for a forest squirrel or chipmunk."

"That's the part where the animals turn to stone," Megan chimed in.

"Little ears hear everything," he whispered.

With a chuckle, Belle twisted, brushing her hand reassuringly up and down Megan's bare, freckled leg. Lovably innocent, she presented an endearing picture in an oversized nautical bucket hat, and Belle found herself wanting to protect her, similar to Andrew's instincts.

"In Narnia," Belle assured Megan, "everything works out for the best."

Leaning back in her seat, Belle recalled that in the play, the children were separated from their mother. Some animals died, as well.

"Megan and I will attend your performance, providing it's a mild version," Andrew was saying.

"It might not be," Belle replied.

He frowned. Belle could see his brilliant mind turning, reviewing the tale.

"In any event," he continued, "I'll be the one clapping the loudest when you take your final bow."

She grinned. "Good to know."

"I enjoy live plays." He brightened. "I especially liked *My Fair Lady*."

"*My Fair Lady* is a musical, not a play."

"Same difference."

"Hardly." Her lips quirked. "But you haven't seen me act yet. You may snatch up your program and dash from the theater at intermission."

"I'll support you no matter what. Good, bad ..." He squeezed her hand. "Exactly as you supported my daughter through her rough times."

THEY REACHED Carolina Beach a half hour later.

"It's illegal to intentionally come within fifty feet of the horses at Corolla," Belle informed Andrew as he opened her door. "We wouldn't have been permitted to feed or pet the horses, anyway."

He gave a thumbs-up. "Best news I've heard all day."

"Daddy!" Megan admonished as he unbuckled her seat belt. "Horses are nice."

"These horses are different, Megan," Belle explained. "Think of them as Honeycrisp's wild cousins."

"They don't faint, do they?" Andrew muttered.

Belle smiled, then drew a wobbly breath. She and Andrew already shared a history of memories and fun, private jokes.

Years earlier, when she'd first acted in minor roles, she'd waited for the director to give her cues. Now, with Andrew, she felt as if she were exactly where she was supposed to be. With him and his daughter. No direction was needed. She just *knew*.

When it came to finding a man she could genuinely love, she hadn't been looking.

But here he was.

A single father. A man of principle. A man who felt real emotions and wasn't ashamed to show them. And she was falling in love with him with a ferocity she could hardly explain.

She brushed her hand against his. "Wild horses don't faint. Only goats. Or women who haven't eaten lunch."

She grinned at his perplexed intake of breath.

"We are grabbing fried scallops later," he said. "Shall we find a place to eat first?"

"Lunch is this afternoon," Belle reminded.

"But we can snack anytime, right, Daddy?" Megan asked. "Didn't you pack corn curls?"

At Belle's lifted eyebrows, he explained, "I'm better with packaged food requiring no preparation."

"Sliced carrots and hummus are nutritious and easy to pack."

"Special days merit special treats."

At his affectionate gaze, her cheeks heated.

Fifteen minutes later, Megan was thoroughly drenched in sunscreen and their beach chairs, towels, and a portable cooler were arranged beside them. Belle and Andrew dug a moat around a castle Megan erected, tamping down wet sand with oversized shovels.

The sky, a brilliant Carolina-blue, mirrored the sunlight and a briny wind whipped across Belle's cheeks. Oftentimes, she'd visualized living near the beach again. Walking barefoot while the waves lapped at her ankles, the golden sand warm and comforting.

And here she was.

"Daddy, can we dive in the water?" Megan, apparently tiring of filling buckets, yanked on Andrew's arm. He held out his hand to Belle although she declined, preferring to lounge on a reclining chair.

She adjusted her sunglasses and easily spotted father and daughter as they splashed in the surf. Andrew's tall, trim body dripped with water, and his drenched swim trunks slicked against his powerful thighs. He had an indisputable magnetism, and she tracked him with her gaze.

Her cellphone pinged, and a text message from her Aunt Lucinda slid across Belle's screen.

How's it going? her aunt inquired.

Alarm prompted Belle to waver. *Are you okay?*

Perfectly fine. I'm sixty, not six hundred.

We're enjoying a day at the beach.

We're?

Andrew and I and Megan.

His daughter? You mention her frequently.

She's precious, Belle responded.

You always wanted children.

Belle touched her throat. Aunt Lucinda invariably stated whatever was on her mind. She had no filter.

Yes, but— Belle began.

I predict you and Andrew will have a big family.

Belle pulled the phone close to her chest. *We've hardly—*

In the meantime, I'm still waiting to meet him.

Dear aunt, I'll arrange something soon. I love you.

I love you. I also love the idea of finding your true partner. Someone to share your joy and sorrow. Do you agree?

Belle nodded, recalling Andrew's song lyric comments. On a promising day like this, love definitely made the world a brighter place.

She snapped her phone shut and shook the sand from her sandals, intending to join Andrew and Megan along the water's edge.

He met her before she'd taken ten steps. She paused, the water fizzing and bubbling at her feet.

"Take a swim," he said. "We'll watch from the shore."

"I'll go in later." With a smile, Belle followed them back to their chairs.

Megan rubbed her eyes, her rosy-red mouth set in a cherubic smile. "Am I a good swimmer?"

Belle gave her a high-five. "The finest on the entire Wilmington shore."

"Sun and water wear her out, although she fights nap time," Andrew mouthed. He wrapped his daughter in a beach towel and tucked her into a chair with an umbrella overhead. Within minutes, the child was asleep.

He slung a towel over his shoulders. Grabbing two water bottles from the cooler, he offered one to Belle. He took a swig of the other and landed on a lounge chair beside her. Their bare feet were so close they almost touched.

"Beach living is the best," he announced.

"You said something similar before. You mentioned surfing—"

He slipped his hand through hers and chuckled. "Do you remember everything I say?"

"Absolutely not." She hid her lie behind an amicable smile and quickly bent her head, concentrating on the water bottle.

"A pity, because I remember everything about you," he murmured.

She reminded herself that Andrew was part of an imaginary life, similar to this brilliant beach day—bold, dazzling and memorable, yet transitory.

He gazed at the ocean. He still held her hand as if he craved her near, craved her touch. She liked that, liked that about him.

"Did I ever tell you about my ex?" he asked.

His serious tone conveyed the importance of the subject.

"A little," she ventured. "You cited the delivery man." She waited for him to offer a Scottish proverb or witty jibe. When he didn't reply, she said softly, "It helps to talk about our concerns."

He nodded. "After Rowena's abrupt departure, Megan was devastated."

"It's only natural. It must have been difficult."

His laugh was brief and grim.

"Rowena didn't give any notice?" Belle asked.

"None. She taped a note to the front door and drove off. We haven't seen her since." Andrew tossed down his water and rested his gaze on Megan.

"How long has Rowena been gone?"

He shifted positions. For several minutes, he focused on the vast expanse of sparkling water reaching the horizon, the sunlight reflecting an intensity of colors.

"Then what happened?" she finally inquired.

Andrew glanced at Belle as if he'd forgotten she sat next

to him. "These past two years she's missed Megan's birthdays and Christmases. I'm the primary custodial parent, and Rowena hasn't contested the lawyer's papers."

"Although I'm sorry for everything, be grateful Megan is in your life." Belle tried to sound untroubled by Rowena's startling lack of interest. "Your daughter adores you and she's happy."

Belle studied the bleak expression on Andrew's face, sensed the somber mood that had descended. Despite his mumble of agreement, he wasn't at peace.

"Don't be sorry for me," he said. "It sounds like this happened all of a sudden, but breakups don't occur in a vacuum. Rowena and I were headed for divorce court several years beforehand." His tone took on a sharp edge. "I can't forgive her."

Belle touched his hand. "Surely, Rowena has attempted to see Megan."

"No," he said shortly. "And selfish is too kind a word to describe her."

Sea gulls cried in the distance, the ocean waves foamy and white. Near them, a group of giggling children made angels in the sand. Carolina Beach was a favorite of Belle's. As a child she'd spent hours wading in the sea spray, and loved the unique, family flavor of the beach and adjacent boardwalk.

She searched her mind for a pleasanter topic rather than dwelling on Andrew's divorce details.

"Ask me anything about Wilmington, and I can answer," she declared with a bright smile.

He wrinkled an eyebrow. "Anything?"

"For instance, the rare Venus flytrap grows here in the wild."

Although his lips were pressed together, a grin slipped through. "I'll keep a look out for it."

"And the flytrap flourishes in a sixty-mile radius around

Wilmington." Belle bobbed her head, delighted and thankful her subject change had worked so swiftly.

"At the risk of dispelling any Venus flytrap myths, if a fly just sits in the trap and doesn't resist, the plant will open, and the fly can leave in the morning," he replied.

"Did you pick up that specific scientific fact from your audiobooks? You are an architect and study … building structures."

"I am. I do. I learned about the Venus flytrap from science *class* in secondary school."

Belle grinned.

She intended to ask more questions—about the bitterness he harbored toward his sister and ex-wife, because she believed she could help him heal.

However, sensitive to the quiet mood, the way it had changed for the better, she held onto the comfortable silence.

The tautness in his jaw relaxed, and she almost missed the genuine affection in his eyes when he smiled at her, because she'd gazed down at their hands, still entwined.

CHAPTER 8

A couple days afterward, Belle stood in her riding ring and announced to Megan, "If it's Monday, it's time for ..."

"Equine therapy!" the little girl chortled as she raced from Andrew's SUV.

"Hurray!" Belle dragged the mounting block to the center of the ring, then bent to secure Megan's pink helmet.

"What about me?" Andrew baited indignantly as he reached the fence.

"Are you wanting a horseback ride?" Belle met his grin with a teasing one beneath her lashes. "Jenkins is in the stable along with Honeycrisp and Felix, my landlord."

"Can I see the horses?" Megan asked.

"Sure," Belle replied, "they're expecting you."

Andrew considered the surroundings. "Where are the goats today?"

"Around."

"Around is a little too vague. I'll stay here." He reached for Belle's arm and shifted her to face him. "First, I'm here to confess that I missed you."

"You confess that a lot."

"Because I think it a lot."

"If you recall, we spent last evening together. Adella watched Megan at your house while we strolled the boardwalk." Belle well remembered the sticky blue blobs of cotton candy she and Andrew had fed each other, the windswept sand dunes, the noisy arcade games lining the two-mile boardwalk. Inside a quaint shop, Andrew had purchased Megan a handmade shell bracelet.

'I like Wilmington,' he'd said to Belle. *'I appreciate the feeling of normality. I tend to forget how valuable leisure time is to a person's health.'*

Belle had agreed in a matter-of-fact voice.

They proceeded, beaming at couples who passed them with affable nods.

"Happily, I finally met your Aunt Lucinda," Andrew was saying.

"Finally." Belle smiled at him. "She prefers living near the boardwalk, so it was an easy walk for us."

"Does she like living close to all these stomach-churning rides?"

"No rides," Belle replied. "Although every Sunday, the Farmer's Market is her chosen spot for homegrown kale. She also shops the adjacent booth for chocolate-covered bacon."

"I suppose healthy cancels out unhealthy when you're sixty years old."

"She buys me bacon too," Belle said. "And I'm not sixty."

He laughed. "So, you like chocolate-covered bacon too?"

"No, but I won't hurt her feelings."

"Let me guess—the bacon is on sale."

"It depends," Belle replied. "I figured out that the man who owns the bacon booth is attracted to her. He becomes all animated when he sees her."

"Vice versa?"

"If I know Aunt Lucinda, it will take more than a pound of chocolate-covered bacon to court her." Belle muffled a laugh. "In any event, you two got along famously when we arrived at her bungalow unannounced."

"She is everything you described and more."

"How much more?"

"Shall I begin with her outfit?" Andrew stifled a grin. "I admit I'm not up-to-date on women's fashion—"

"You object to her Indiana Jones hat?"

"I was prepared for the hat. For her remarks, not so much."

Belle paused. "Aunt Lucinda doesn't mince words."

"I noticed."

"She likes you."

"I like her too. I especially like what she suggested."

"Who's Aunt Lucinda?" Megan bounded up to them. "What did she say, daddy?"

Belle's cheeks burned as Andrew extended a helpless smile. Aunt Lucinda had given Andrew the once-over and candidly declared he was exactly the man Belle was destined to marry.

Andrew had agreed, pulling Belle into his arms and kissing her. Belle had returned his kiss with all the love brimming in her heart.

Because Andrew had agreed.

"Aunt Lucinda is Miss Belle's aunt. Soon, you'll meet her." He kissed Megan on the cheek and looped an arm around Belle's waist.

A HALF HOUR LATER, Megan finished her therapy session, and Felix offered to bring Megan to the stable to unsaddle Honeycrisp, then turn the horses out to pasture.

"I'm in town all week," Andrew said, when Belle met him

at the fence. "Will dinner and a movie at my place suffice for a date?"

"More than suffice."

"I can stream Braveheart."

"So you're in a sentimental mood and reminiscing about Scotland." Belle opened the gate and stepped over to him. "Are you serving haggis?"

"Are you brave enough to sample a plate?"

"You mentioned your sister makes the best haggis. Next, you'll probably charter a private jet to Scotland to see her."

He rubbed his hands over his face. "Nope."

"Potatoes and turnips will do, then. Both are favorite Scottish dishes."

"You've done your Scottish homework." His mouth tilted at the corners. "I assume it's because you were eager to learn more about me?"

Thinking of an excuse to refute his claim, she ended up simply nodding. There was no sense hiding her feelings. He knew she was interested.

He just didn't know how much, because she was unquestionably, unequivocally falling in love with him.

"I'll ask Adella to prepare a Scottish meal for us." He rubbed his palm against Belle's cheek and grinned. "When we watch Braveheart, be prepared to see some of the most gorgeous scenery you'll ever witness."

The ache of longing in his voice for his homeland tugged at her. She squeezed her eyes shut as his fingers wandered to stroke her hair.

He missed Scotland. He should resolve the issues with his sister. There was no purpose in holding onto a grudge. What was the Scottish phrase?

"You're a long time deid," she murmured.

The grin vanished from his features. "What did you say?" He dropped his hand and stared at her.

"Nothing."

"You're parroting one of my Scottish sayings?"

"They're not *your* sayings, they're your country's sayings, and you should embrace them. Life is short. Forgive your ex. Forgive your sister."

"Why?"

"It's obvious. Forgiveness will set you free."

He glanced toward the stable before fixing his gaze on Belle. "Sometimes there are too many wrongs to right."

"Forgiving the people who may have wronged you will provide peace of mind."

"I am at peace."

"Are you?"

"You're an equine therapist, Belle, not a human therapist." His brief smile didn't reach his eyes. "If I need advice, I'll check a self-help book out of the library."

She recoiled, but pushed on. "Begin the process of healing. Do it for yourself."

Instead of agreeing, he stared past her.

"Furthermore, Andrew," she touched his arm, "you work too much."

"Thanks for the advice. Unfortunately, this isn't a good time for a psychological discussion."

"When? When is a good time?"

He brought up a hand, interrupting her with utter finality. "Let's put this conversation behind us."

Belle held her tongue, quelling her reflexive reaction to offer more suggestions.

His cellphone buzzed. He read the text and frowned.

"What is it?" she asked.

"There is trouble in Camden. A resident was hurt, and they're blaming the accident on the worksite not being properly secured and safe." He blew out a breath as Megan emerged from the stable. "Let's take a raincheck, okay?"

Belle didn't respond, and he hardly noticed as he signaled to Megan that they were leaving. He brushed a kiss on Belle's forehead as he passed, murmuring an assurance that he would text her as soon as he arrived in Camden.

She waited. Surely he would turn back to her, so she could suggest that he stay.

Maybe he would ponder his quick decision. Maybe he would declare that his foreman could easily handle any problems.

But he didn't, and neither did she, swallowing her protests because they were futile.

Knowing he would refuse, anyway.

CHAPTER 9

*B*elle braced a hand on the window frame over her kitchen sink, and admired the purple zinnias flowering in the garden, the whitish-gray bark of an oak tree, the sun setting on another September day.

Summer was over, and so was her romance with Andrew.

That is, if it had ever begun.

Andrew. First in her thoughts, first in her heart.

They'd been friends before their relationship had deepened to romance. Good friends, confidantes, really. She could tell him anything.

But love was elusive. Yes, there were moments made just for them—the boardwalk, the sunsets, the shared laughter.

Followed by longer moments, like today, when she felt utterly alone.

The beautiful dahlias he'd gifted had died, and she'd replaced the flowers with a ceramic bowl of fake oranges.

Andrew. With him, she believed she'd found a genuine love. A deep connection, both large and small. In his arms, she was beloved and cherished.

She shook her head. She'd been so wrong.

She suppressed her heart's disloyal leap whenever she envisioned Andrew's striking features, his enthralling smile, his endearing Scottish brogue.

Forcibly reminding herself that he was gone, she brewed peppermint tea in a glass mug and claimed a kitchen chair.

Andrew was content expanding his architecture firm and raising his daughter. What more did he need?

When he Skyped Belle from Camden a few minutes later, Belle told him as much.

"That's your version of a hello?" His features sharpened beneath the brash overhead light of his hotel room.

"You left the riding ring quickly the other day," she answered.

"Belle, there is a lot going on here. I can't deal with any more guilt—if that's where this conversation is headed." Although his words were firm, there was no harshness. His tone with her and his daughter was always kind, gentle and respectful.

By now, however, Belle understood the rules, his rules. He'd made them clear. Don't discuss his life, his choices, his priorities.

"In any case, will you heed my advice?" she pressed.

"Which is?"

"Appreciate your life. You employ a large staff and shouldn't do everything yourself." She took a deep breath. "Not to mention you carry a heavy burden you should confront."

Immediately, she regretted her outburst when his features became firm and unbending.

"Are you trying to fix me?" he asked.

"No. Well, yes, maybe. I can't understand your unreasonable work ethic. You love your daughter, yet you leave her alone constantly."

"I've provided a magnificent home, enrolled Megan in an

exclusive private school, and bought her a horse. Aside from that, Adella is an excellent caretaker."

"Still, you should—"

"I need … I should…" He shot her a wearied look. "I am who I am."

She stared at the phone screen as he looked away. When she caught his gaze again, his eyes glistened. With frustration? Unshed tears? Now she wasn't certain he'd handled their discussion as dismissively as she'd assumed.

I love you, which is why I'm trying to help you, she wanted to tell him, but his manner became patronizing when he inserted, "I'm older than you, remember? Be a good equine therapist and don't worry about fixing a jaded architect like me."

"You're right, then. I won't." Her chin came up. "And it's time I resume my quiet life with my animals."

"What are you saying?"

"I'm ending our discussion, Andrew. The horses need to come in from the pasture."

Her wounded pride wouldn't permit her to say anymore.

"Right now?" he asked irritably. "All day I looked forward to talking to you. It was what got me through a very wearying meeting with the Camden town council."

"Sorry, but you'll need to conduct both ends of our conversation because I'm clicking off."

"I'll phone you tomorrow night."

"Rehearsals are beginning for The Lion, The Witch, and the Wardrobe."

"So you got a role? Are you Mrs. Beaver?"

"I'm a forest animal."

"Which one?"

"A squirrel."

"That's nuts. Get it?"

She couldn't suppress her grin, though her heart was

breaking. She'd miss his wit and Scottish phrases, but she'd made up her mind. A long-distance relationship that relied on his unpredictable work schedule would never be successful.

"I'll be back in Wilmington on Saturday," he said. "Dinner at my place?"

His simple request almost brought her to tears. She tugged her gaze from the cellphone screen, grappling with the desolate mood settling over her. It took all her limited acting skills to summon a spirited attitude as she uttered a final goodbye.

When he clicked off, her breath pushed out in a rush. She'd never see his home again, never watch a sunset with him, never experience his tender kisses.

She struggled to control the agonizing tug in her heart.

But she failed, put her head in her hands, and wept.

IN TYPICAL ANDREW FASHION, he texted daily, updating her on his work progress before declaring the problem in Camden was solved and he would return to Wilmington by the weekend.

He didn't, and one week became two, then three. Days merged into weeks, and the end of September loomed. The weather remained sticky-hot as the final days of torrid temperatures descended on the Southern beachfront town.

Although Belle continued seeing Megan, and Adella briefed her on Andrew's whereabouts, the sessions weren't the same.

With a wobbly smile, Belle responded to Adella's updates with a cheerful acknowledgement.

To Andrew's credit, he communicated with her often, although she continuously cut him off. Instead of wasting the hours alone, she immersed herself in caring for the horses, her clients' therapy sessions, and nightly play rehearsals.

Aunt Lucinda had little doubt behind the reasons for Belle's ceaseless round of activity, but as their afternoon at the Sunday Farmer's Market faded into twilight, her worried glances whenever Belle became teary-eyed when Andrew's name was mentioned came less often. And even her aunt wasn't bold enough to continue asking why Belle no longer would discuss the man she loved.

There were mornings when Belle didn't contemplate how her life would have been with Andrew, evenings when she didn't revisit his texts, and dawns when she didn't lie awake staring listlessly out the window, recalling his Scottish brogue as he whispered loving words to her.

Nevertheless, those days were few.

"How is Andrew?" Candee inquired when she phoned Belle one evening.

Belle settled on the living room couch with the cat stretched out beside her. "He's still in Camden, I think."

"You *think* he's in Camden? Where else would he be? Don't you trust him?"

"Of course. It's just—"

"There isn't a man who works harder, except for my husband Teddy, or Rob, or Kieran."

Belle murmured a concession at Candee's fierce protectiveness of Andrew, as well as all the other men in her life. Teddy worked alongside his crewmen on job sites, plus flipped homes. Rob assisted his wife, Kathleen, at her teahouse. Beforehand, he'd owned several bakeries, Rob's Marvelous Muffins, in Florida. Kieran, who had married Candee's sister, Desiree, ran an Irish pub in Roses. In all three cases, the wives were supportive of their husbands' endeavors.

Why couldn't Belle do the same?

To begin with, she and Andrew weren't married, much less engaged. He'd never declared his love for her, not in so many words.

"Andrew is consumed with his business and when he isn't, he deserves to spend any precious free hours with his daughter," Belle responded. "Which is, of course, as it should be."

"Should it be? Why?"

Belle sighed. "I don't know if he loves me enough to spend time with me, anyway."

"You're being absurd. From what I understand, he spends every spare moment with you when he's in Wilmington. Has he texted you?"

"Constantly."

"And?"

"I hardly respond. What's the use? I can't depend on him, because, well, he's never here."

Candee cleared her throat. "First, I can assure you that he's in love with you. The look on his face when he visited me in Roses a few weeks ago ... well ... he's completely enamored with you, Belle."

"Candee, you're a true friend, but you're wrong."

"Andrew keeps to himself. Did you know his family moved to America with literally nothing?"

Belle didn't respond.

"Give him a chance. Accept his phone calls and texts. He's a complex man."

And brilliant, Belle thought. And sensitive, honest, and attentive.

Still ...

"I can't." A quiet dignity firmed Belle's assertion. "I don't understand his intense drive to succeed. What is he proving? He's accumulated a fortune already."

"It's not about the money, Belle. His father lost his business, his wealth, and that left an impression on Andrew. Teddy and I have discussed him at length."

"Someone should tell Andrew to stop working so much."

"A Type A personality rarely listens to good advice, or any advice, for that matter."

With a ragged laugh, Belle agreed. "Even if he heeded our suggestions, I won't take him away from his daughter."

"He has enough love for both you and Megan, just as I love Teddy and Joseph."

Belle tried not to listen to Candee's words. She'd continue to push Andrew Bransfield out of her heart, out of her life, by ignoring him.

And by doing so, she had never felt as forlorn.

"By the way," Candee was saying, "Andrew purchased the Wilmington house he was renting."

Disregarding the lump in her throat at the realization he would live only a few blocks away, Belle sat up. "He did? When?"

"A week ago. Sorry. He may have intended to spill the news as a surprise."

Through a sheen of tears, Belle pulled her knees to her chest.

Firmly, she repeated to herself that she had no reason to be angry just because Andrew Bransfield was moving forward with his life, while her life had stalled.

So, she continued to ride her finicky horse, nurture the animals, and treat her therapy clients with fastidious care. She'd put herself in neutral; an emotional balance she maintained, ensuring she'd shed no more tears over him. It was better this way, ending the relationship slowly, with no confrontation.

. . .

WHEN ANDREW RETURNED to Wilmington the following Friday evening, he texted Belle and invited her to his home for takeout dinner and a movie.

She declined.

He suggested a Saturday boardwalk date, but she declined, citing the excuse of busyness.

"Right. Okay." She visualized his frown as he accepted her refusal. "Shall we try for Sunday? There's a Mexican restaurant serving the best—"

Before he finished, she made up an explanation about studying her script, although they both knew her part in The Lion, The Witch, and The Wardrobe had no words.

It hardly mattered, because he texted her on Monday. He was leaving for another job site in the Carolinas.

A PATTERN FORMED as the days drifted through the month of October. He'd text her, and she'd respond with quick one-sentences.

How are you? he'd ask.

Good. You?

The same. Equine therapy still on for Monday? I will finally be in town for a while. Can we have dinner together? There's a new Italian place in town.

Sorry. Too busy, she texted. *Opening night is next Friday.*

Finally. These play rehearsals have gone on forever. Did you nail your infamous role as a squirrel?

Soundly. Complete with a white vinyl tail and furry gray mitts.

Can't wait to see you.

Perform? Visit her? He knew where she lived. She didn't touch that one, instead replying with, *Can't. Rehearsals are till ten PM.*

Through the weeks of correspondence, he'd finish his

texts with smiling emojis, flashing red or pink hearts. Tonight he concluded with a questioning face.

CHAPTER 10

*W*hat was more exciting, more intoxicating, more nerve-wracking, than opening night at a theater? It hardly mattered if the production was professional or amateur, the thrill, the rush, was the same.

Belle adjusted the tail on her squirrel costume and peeked at the audience as the curtain raised. The Lion, The Witch, and The Wardrobe had sold out for both weekend nights, and the crowded community theater shifted with anticipation. Posters hung in various businesses, in addition to the announcements on local radio stations, and the advertisements had proved beneficial. The director insisted on staying true to the book, incessantly occupied with the imaginative sets and choreography.

Belle searched the rows for Aunt Lucinda, who had arranged to meet her backstage afterwards, but didn't spot her. In many instances, her aunt had made a late grand entrance, so not seeing her wasn't cause for alarm.

Aunt Lucinda had mentioned bringing a surprise. Perhaps the right man for her had come along after all … perhaps the man from the Farmer's Market?

Belle ducked into the hallway, the canned music began, and the narrator intoned:

"Once there were ..."

THE TWO-AND-A-HALF HOURS of the play passed in an exhilarating blur. Afterwards, Belle hugged and congratulated the actors and actresses, then reported to her makeshift dressing room. Settled on a stool in front of a mirror, she yanked off her mitts and scrubbed away her face make-up while she waited for her aunt.

Muted voices made her pause. Aunt Lucinda's voice, followed by her larger-than-life laugh, announced she was near.

But it was the other voice, a rich Scottish brogue, that forced Belle slowly to her feet. This man was not the bacon shopkeeper, nor the suave, sophisticated Andrew of her dreams. This Andrew was an irresistible force. As he rounded the corner, his rugged features were torn between distress and tenderness.

He was real. He was here.

ANDREW DIDN'T HEAR Aunt Lucinda, nor the performers they passed in the hallway. He was already striding into a cramped dressing room, packed with discarded water bottles, headphones and a clothes rack jammed with costumes.

Belle stood by a mirror, holding a cloth in one hand, a pair of furry gray mitts in the other.

Entranced, he remained by the doorway, observing her radiant smile as her aunt scurried forward, holding her arms wide for a congratulatory hug.

He advanced, standing five feet away from Belle. He kept

his hands at his sides, clutching the flowers he'd brought. He was uncertain what to say, how to move.

He stared at her freshly scrubbed face, devoid of make-up, her dove-gray eyes filled with tears. The eyes that had gripped his nightly dreams and consumed his daytime thoughts.

He hadn't the slightest notion if she still cared for him. Or worse, had she forgotten all about him? He hadn't known what kind of reception he would receive from her when he'd phoned her aunt, requesting a ticket to the production.

Or, if he could now prove to Belle that he was worthy of sharing her life.

Her aunt gave them both a look of profound satisfaction. "Say what you came here for, Andrew, before Belle starts to cry."

His gaze trained on Belle's delicate face as he set down the flowers and wiped his eyes. "I'll cry with her."

"Men don't cry." Aunt Lucinda clucked her tongue. "Especially strong Scottish men."

"Dear aunt, you've been watching too much Braveheart," Belle said, as she rushed into his arms.

He cradled her, shielding her from her aunt's observant stare.

"I missed you," he whispered, knowing Aunt Lucinda heard every word, and not caring.

"You always say that," Belle replied.

"I couldn't figure out any other way to see you. Adella agreed to watch Megan, although Megan wanted to come. I wasn't sure about this production, though."

"It's okay. Next time. Andrew, I love your little girl."

He smiled. Belle carried enough love for everyone.

"If I asked you out again," he continued, "I assumed you would make up another excuse to avoid me."

She gazed up at him. "What's better than tonight, coupled

with my triumph as a squirrel?" She grinned, but then her shoulders shook with sobs as she glided her hands around his neck, and snuggled her tear-stained face close to his chest.

Her aunt's sing-song voice made them both jump. "I'm grabbing a bite to eat and headed home. Well done, Belle. Your performance did me proud."

"All thirty seconds of my debut."

"You were the prettiest squirrel on stage," came Aunt Lucinda's reply.

Belle brought her head up and offered her aunt a dry smile. "I was also the *only* squirrel on stage."

Andrew grinned. "Thank you, Aunt Lucinda." He hesitated. "May I call you my aunt?"

"You're welcome. And now that you've finally come to your senses, then yes."

He kept Belle firmly in his arms. Desperate to be alone with her, he speculated how to politely ask her aunt to leave without being blunt.

Aunt Lucinda caught his uneasy gaze. "It's a jubilant day when two people find true partners to share their lives." At the far end of the room, she switched the lights to dim, and was gone.

Belle stepped back and regarded him. "I still can't believe you're here. An hour earlier, I felt so desolate and—"

"Hollow?" he provided. "Unfulfilled?"

"And yet, you came to my performance."

"Because musicals are my favorite."

"The Lion, The Witch, and the Wardrobe is a play."

"Right." He picked up the flowers. "I bought these dahlias for you. They're a bit wilted."

She accepted, sniffed, and clutched the bouquet to her chest. "They're beautiful. Thank you."

"Why are you crying again?"

"Because I know ... I know what they mean."

"A commitment shared forever by two persons." He took her slender hand in his. "Belle Boots, I love you."

She answered with her lips, parting them as he stroked her luxurious hair. She responded with the same ardor as when they'd kissed at his home, the night of the sunset.

Then she pulled away. "Can we talk?" she asked, her gaze honest and direct.

"Now?"

"Now is the best time."

"I forgot you're as blunt as your aunt."

"Andrew, I love you, but you're always working."

"Not anymore." Somehow, he managed to control his tone, recalling the weight that had been lifted from him when he'd come to his decision. "I offered my main foreman more responsibility, and he accepted. We've worked together for years, and I trust him."

"That's so encouraging. But there's more, Andrew. For your sake, can you find it in your heart to forgive your sister?"

"I can't."

"You can, with me standing beside you."

"What is it about you that brings out the best in me?"

Her hand tightened on his arm. "So you might reach out to Kate?"

"These things take time, but I will try."

"Thank you." Her infectious laugh that had lightened his days conveyed a trace of innocence. "And there's one more thing."

"More?"

"What about horses?"

"What about them?" Distracted, he kissed her, relishing

the delicious combination of joy and love she brought to his heart.

"Will you venture into the riding ring with me, when the horses are there?"

"Under one condition."

"Which is?"

"Will you marry me?"

"You're bartering horses with an offer of marriage?"

"Exactly."

"Then yes." She nodded, replying with the response he'd waited for.

"I can't guarantee I'll stay in the ring for more than a minute," he warned. "But I expect our marriage will last a lifetime."

"I know it will." She lifted her delicate eyebrows in a challenge. "I also know that you and Jenkins will get along. He's an excellent judge of character."

"Does that mean he'll like me?"

"If you're a beginning rider, then yes."

"How did we go from entering a ring, to actually riding a horse?"

She stood on her toes and kissed him. "We'll take it slow."

He reached into his pocket and handed her a program. "I wrote a poem." On the back of the program, he'd written in large letters, "You're the woman I want, you're the woman I need."

She scanned the words. "You write poems," she said quietly. "Why am I not surprised?"

"Not very good ones because they don't rhyme, but yes." He held her close, reciting the last two lines of his poem with her:

"Because in the end, it's all about love."

And he sealed his words in Scottish Gaelic.

"Tha-mi-gad-ghradh."
I love you.

THE END

A NOTE FROM JOSIE

Dear Friend,

Thank you for spending the summer in Roses and Wilmington with Belle and Andrew.

1-800-SUMMER is the fourth book in my Flipping for You series. Belle's story gave me an excuse to research a world I knew nothing about, and I fell completely in love with it. Equine therapy is a fascinating, deeply moving field, and I hope I did it justice on the pages.

The series continues with *1-800-NEW YEAR*, where Lincoln and Shanice get their story, and wraps up with *Christmas in the Air* — a holiday romance about a single mother and the new pediatrician in town.

If Belle and Andrew's story moved you, I'd be so grateful if you'd leave a review. Every review helps another reader find a book they'll love.

1-800-SUMMER is available in ebook, paperback, large print, hardcover, and audiobook.

I started writing because I was afraid to and it mattered too much to risk. Whatever you've been putting off for that same reason: do it anyway. The risk is worth it.

With sincere gratitude,

Josie Riviera

My Spotify Play List for 1-800-SUMMER is here.

Want more of the 1-800-Series, Flipping For You?
Click here.

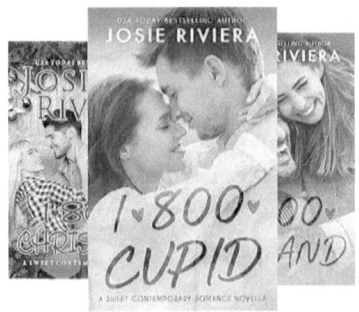

Or grab the 1-800-Series Collection.
The entire series! 6 sweet romances in 1 giant boxed set.

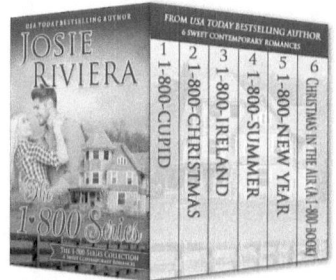

KATE'S OLD FAMILY
HAGGIS RECIPE

Ingredients:

1 lb. lean mutton - ground

1 pound chopped suet

1 lb. organ meat (lungs, liver, heart) (chicken livers work well)

6 onions peeled & chopped finely

1 tsp. salt

1 pint liquid

¼ tsp thyme, ¼ tsp coriander, ¼ tsp savory, ¼ tsp. marjoram, ¼ tsp nutmeg, ¼ tsp basil, 1 tsp garlic powder (or fresh garlic, chopped), ½-1 tsp freshly ground black pepper, ½ tsp cayenne pepper, 1 bay leaf

2 cups finely ground oatmeal, toasted (make sure you toast it. This step makes a big difference.)

Stomach bag of sheep or muslin bag. (You can use an oven bag - like those you use to roast a turkey.) If you don't use the sheep stomach, dissolve 2 crushed rennet tablets in water and add to the meat mixture.

Preparation:

Wash the stomach bag in cold saltwater. Boil organ meats for 1 ½ hours, leaving windpipe attached to lungs & hanging out of the pot. Impurities will drip out, so put a pan underneath. Cool. Cutaway windpipe skin, & gristle. Put aside some of the liquid in which the organ meats were boiled. Mince organ meats & add to other meat & suet. Toast oatmeal in the oven and add to meat mixture with chopped onion and spices. Add enough liquid from boiled organ meats to make a soft consistency.

If you use a sheep stomach or muslin bag, fill a little more than half full. Close tightly, prick, and put into a pan of boiling water with a plate at the bottom. Boil 3-4 hours. Prick occasionally to stop bag from bursting.

If you use an oven bag, put in an aluminum pan on top of a baking sheet. Kind of pat the bag flat. Turn and mix periodically until it looks done. Timing depends on how much you make and when it looks done.

And the most important part, the oven temperature!

Serves 8-10   Oven temp 325-350 (if you bake it)

BONUS: SNEAK PEEK
AT 1-800-NEW YEAR

Chapter One

I think I fancy you.

Shanice Williams sat in her rustic farmhouse kitchen,

absorbed by the text flashing across the dating app on her cell phone.

She'd received a private message from Todd.

She kneaded her forehead and sighed.

Todd who?

And he *fancied* her? How? He'd never even met her.

She winced. Surely there were better pickup lines.

While she searched her brain for a suitable response, she peered out the window over the sink. The early morning sun rose higher in the sky, illuminating the fields. The timbered barn was located on the hill beyond, its green metal roof gleaming. A khaki-colored stone firepit sat nearby. Feathery snow powdered the grass, confirming the December wintry weather.

Still there? Todd inquired.

She didn't reply.

At the suggestion of Candee Winchester, her friend and Realtor, Shanice had joined Cupid Aplenty, a dating website, and uploaded a selfie. In the photo, her dark skin glowed, enhanced by a brush of deep-pink blusher, and her headful of black hair peeked from beneath her trademark white beanie. The words, "A Patch of Heaven," the name of her landscaping company, were embroidered on the brim in vivid green.

"I'm a professional landscaper. Consequently, I appreciate the outdoors," she'd described herself. "Faith in God is important, as well as family, friends, and old-fashioned morals. I own a super cute cat who is often erratic and reckless, and I'm an animal lover. Oh, and my ideal match is a knight in shining armor with scruples and ethics."

Still there? Todd asked again.

Unsure how to respond, she scanned his profile.

Todd Herring. A normal-looking fellow flashing a

mouthful of dazzling white teeth. His shaggy blond hair glistened with platinum highlights.

Did he dye his hair? She speculated on that while another of his texts rolled in.

I bet my new kitten would really like your cat.

She wasn't certain whether to laugh or cry.

Do you have a favorite indoor restaurant, or are you the outdoorsy type? he asked.

Huh?

Twice, she reread his question. Apparently, Todd had zeroed in on her cat and ignored her profession.

Outdoorsy, she typed.

Wanna go on a date sometime?

Her fingers hovered over the phone's keyboard. Why, oh why, had she joined an online dating service? Was she that desperate?

The recent breakup with her on-again, off-again boyfriend, Brian, had been difficult. They'd grown apart, and she'd never felt as if he actually listened to her or valued what she'd accomplished. Besides, he wasn't the type of guy who liked to stay in one place. He preferred to travel, whereas she was a homebody.

Candee insisted Shanice was a romantic at heart—pointing out her fondness for reading sweet romance books.

People took solace in different things. For some, it was eating comfort food, such as meat loaf and mashed potatoes, or chocolate, or wintergreen puff candy. Shanice favored the optimism, promise and happy outcomes of romantic novels.

"Online dating eliminates awkward first dates," Candee had encouraged.

Shanice preferred face-to-face interaction rather than communicating through a phone or computer screen. In addition, she always deferred to her gut reaction.

She gazed at Todd's photo grinning up at her and went

with her gut. *I can't commit, but thanks for the invite,* she replied.

Polite and done. Then she hit the delete button, blocking Todd from contacting her again.

Well, that was quite an adventure, and it wasn't even seven o'clock in the morning.

She padded to the refrigerator and poured a glass of sweet iced tea.

She hadn't mastered the art of refusal. In fact, dating in general had never been her forte. Not since she'd attended community college fifteen years earlier and met the most wonderful man imaginable.

"A girl never gets over her first love," Granny had once declared. "Especially a smart, handsome guy like Lincoln Reid. Shanice, that boy is clearly in love with you."

Shanice ran a hand across her brow. Everyone knew Jasmine Williams was an authority on most everything. A widow at twenty-six, Jasmine had managed to purchase several acres and a rundown farm, hired farmhands, and eventually turned a profit. She was tenacious, independent, and more than a little impulsive. As a black woman living alone in a sleepy Blue Ridge Mountain town, those qualities had served her well.

Only after Jasmine's second husband died unexpectedly did her health decline. Sadness had taken its toll on Shanice's eighty-five-year-old grandmother.

"Of course a person gets over their first love, Granny," Shanice said aloud. Wasn't she proof? She'd carried on, hadn't she?

Admittedly, she'd combed for Lincoln on the internet, always regretting her searches afterwards because she could never find him.

It was high time to get over him, she told herself. In any case, she'd come to the conclusion he didn't use social media.

She set down her glass and softly sang "Go Tell It on the Mountain." She'd committed every word of the song to memory. She'd attempted to teach the lyrics to Lincoln, though he'd invariably mixed up the words, changing "over the hills," to "over the mountains."

"No, Lincoln. It's a hill, not a mountain. There's a difference." At his grimace and half-shrug, they'd laugh. Christmas had held so much fun, so much joy.

So much anticipation.

Up until the day she died, Granny had sung hymns. In years past, Shanice had embraced Christmas celebrations, but this December was different—lonelier and sadder with Granny gone.

They'd always been a dynamic twosome.

Wherever Shanice went on the farm, every room smelled like Granny's fragrance—fragrant gardenias—in the kitchen, the bedrooms and even the outdoor gardens.

Perhaps that was why Lincoln was in her thoughts today. She was emotional amidst all the festivities and no one to share it with.

"Go tell it on …" The hymn stalled on her lips. "Granny, I'm sorry, but I need to sell the farmhouse. Jasmine's Joy is a splendid name for a house with a proud legacy, though I'm not the person to carry the legacy into the next generation. All the labor and money needed for restoration are beyond my expertise and limited funds."

Shanice ran her hands across the plaid curtains hanging over the sink, and then the plate racks displaying chipped, flowered blue china dishes. Her sad excuse for holiday decorations—a gingerbread cookie jar, circa 1970—occupied a space on the enamel kitchen table.

According to Candee, selling and then closing on the farmhouse by New Year's Day allowed enough time for the paperwork to be signed and a check issued, enabling Shanice to pay for her next loan installment.

Due January 30.

Her hands fell to her sides. Her landscaping business wasn't bringing in sufficient funds to provide for everyday expenses, let alone cover loan payments.

She sat back down. Her tortoiseshell cat, a "tortie" she'd adopted from a pet rescue center years ago, jumped on her lap.

"What can we do, Duchess?" Shanice stroked the cat's patch-colored fur and a throaty purring rewarded her. "I'm in a hurry and forced to sell the house 'as is.'"

Fortunately, there was no mortgage and minimal property taxes. Her grandmother's will had only stipulated she live in the house for three months before deciding whether she'd sell.

A rather odd request.

Still, she'd agreed, because three months flew by quickly. Moreover, she'd often called the farmhouse her "castle in the air," because the ramble of rooms resembled a miniature castle. Add the intricate woodwork and stone tile, and all the house needed was a Prince Charming.

Subleasing her rather boring apartment in Huntington, an adjacent town, she'd honored her grandmother's final request and moved to Roses, North Carolina. She'd intended to modernize the house in her free time.

Hah! Shanice soon discovered she had none. She managed to update one bathroom—an absolute necessity—and painted the upstairs room she'd chosen for her bedroom a lovely light blue. The extra seven rooms were closed off to conserve on the utility bills. She hadn't gotten around to staining the wood trim, nor did she have the means to fix the old radiators that struggled to keep the place warm.

Her cell phone rang.

"Hi," Candee said before Shanice uttered a greeting. "I haven't heard from the potential buyer scheduled to view your house today."

"The showing is for ten o'clock, correct?"

"Precisely. He's a last-minute buyer."

"Is he dependable?" Shanice asked.

"I don't know. He was supposed to drive from Hilton Head Island early this morning. Plus, we've never met."

"Does he live on Hilton Head?"

"I believe so."

"Why is he interested in a house a few hours away?"

"He claims he used to live here. However, with this unexpected cold snap and being the day after Christmas, I suspect he'll cancel."

"Fingers crossed he'll make an offer."

"He'll need to see the house first." Candee chuckled. "May I remind you that you refused two offers last month?"

"Because both were insultingly low." Shanice cuddled her cat closer to her chest. "I want a fair price because this house meant the world to Granny. In addition, my finances are nonexistent."

"But you said your landscaping business is profitable. That'll help."

"Fall cleanups were a blessing, but winter is the slow season."

"The right buyer will come along." Candee hesitated. "How was your Christmas?"

"Quiet. I attended church, then volunteered at the food bank in town serving roasted turkey with all the trimmings."

"Teddy and I hoped you'd reconsidered our invite to share Christmas dinner with us. Joseph has a new horse he wants to show you—a Shetland pony, and we have beagles running all over the place. Plus, I have landscaping questions. I want to redo my front lawn, and I'd appreciate an estimate."

Candee had met her husband, Teddy, when he visited Roses searching for a real estate investment. They'd married and adopted Joseph, Teddy's nephew. Joseph's father had died in a horrific car accident. His mother had died a year earlier.

"I'll provide a landscaping quote when I visit," Shanice replied. "Lawns in the south are best overhauled in the spring or fall."

"Desiree and Keiran stopped by yesterday and brought their infamous pistachio cake," Candee added. "They still act as if they're newlyweds."

"They're adorable together," Shanice said.

"Love and romance are in the air during the holidays."

Shanice winced. Maybe for other people. Certainly not for her.

She glanced toward the living room. Besides the cookie jar, her only other attempt at festive decorations was a one-foot potted fir tree, which she'd trimmed with African-themed ornaments she found in the attic. Likewise, she'd decorated her sponsored tree for Roses' annual Festival of Trees event. The tree was sparse, though Candee had assured her it looked effortlessly chic, which was all the rage.

Shanice also observed Kwanzaa, a cultural holiday cele-brated along with her Christian Christmas. Today, December twenty-sixth, marked the beginning of that week-long cele-bration.

She'd placed an African cloth, a mat, an ear of corn, pieces of fruit, and seven candles on a bureau. The corn represented fertility, the fruit brought happiness and perseverance. She planned on lighting the first candle later in the evening.

Granny had used those same trimmings and Kwanzaa decorations year after year.

"No use in buying new when old is just as good," she would declare, tossing her gray braids over her shoulders.

"Cash is better spent on farm equipment and keeping Jasmine's Joy afloat."

Granny was an expert on pinching a dollar. She'd taught Shanice how to shop at thrift stores for the best bargains.

I haven't changed a thing, she silently told her grandmother, *although I did purchase seven new candles. Candles don't expire, but there wasn't enough wax in the old ones to melt and reuse.*

Her cat leapt from her arms, spotting a bird by the living room window. She'd set up a birdwatching station in the yard, and Duchess spent hours watching cardinals and chickadees fly to the feeders.

"I'll continue to schedule showings while you're at work," Candee was saying, bringing Shanice back to the present.

"I'm stopping by the Festival of Trees to view my tree before the event is dismantled."

"Your tree is gorgeous," Candee continued. "The zebra ornaments and African American angel topper are so elegant."

"The decorations were Granny's, and I donated the six-foot artificial balsam fir. This was my way to honor her legacy."

"She would've been proud," Candee said. "Your tree commanded the highest bid at the online auction."

"Really? Who bought the tree?"

"A mysterious bidder from out of town."

"Hmm." Shanice paused. "I wonder who."

"Don't know."

"Most important, the funds go toward the town's senior food program," Shanice said.

Granny had relied on that program, which provided a daily healthy hot meal. At first, she'd protested, declaring her independence, but Shanice had insisted and arranged the service. It brought her peace of mind because she'd discouraged her grandmother from using the stove or microwave. In the final weeks, she'd hired full-time care since she wasn't always able to get to town.

Her grandmother had refused to move from the farmhouse and live with Shanice.

As the year had passed, the corn crop went unplanted. The sheep and goats had eventually been sold. All that remained were four chickens. Granny would sit for hours by the fireplace, an afghan pulled snugly to her chin.

"I'm getting another call," Candee said.

"Any likelihood it's the Hilton Head buyer? Feel free to bring him and a conga line of other prospective purchasers around. I'm eager for a quick closing and cash is best."

Candee laughed. "My job and my pleasure."

Shanice clicked off as another call rang through. She recognized the caller ID of MaryEllen, an elderly woman and Granny's dearest friend.

"May I ask a favor?" MaryEllen inquired. "Can you stop by my place and throw down ice melt so I can get to my Monday lunch at the women's club this afternoon?"

"I'll be over within the hour."

As Shanice disconnected, Duchess jumped onto her favorite perch, a worn green sofa. The sofa was serviceable, though it had faded and bleached after forty years of service.

Shanice shrugged on a cream-colored Sherpa parka, gloves, her knitted white beanie, and tucked her jeans into sturdy work boots. She snatched a handful of wintergreen peppermint puffs from a glass jar. No holiday was complete without a sweet candy that melted in your mouth.

A minute later, she started her blue pickup truck and drove several miles to MaryEllen's apartment complex. When Shanice arrived, she responded to calls from other customers requesting the same service, breathing a sense of relief for the extra money the jobs brought in.

If only she could sell her house for a fair price, secure her business loan, and return to her Huntington apartment.

At noon, her hands shaking from exhaustion, she pulled her truck to the rear of the farmhouse and worked off her gloves. She hadn't mustered the energy to visit the Festival of Trees, and assured herself she had until tomorrow to see her exquisitely decorated tree before it was claimed and taken away by the winning bidder.

She rubbed her jeans, damp with snow, and bit back a groan. How could she have slipped and fallen on the icy sidewalk at MaryEllen's house? A peril from outdoor tasks, she supposed.

Since then, her hip and knee smarted. She stepped onto the back entrance that led to the kitchen, envisioning a warm Epsom-salt soak in the antique, cast-iron bathtub.

As she opened the door, a man's voice gave her pause.

"I'm thinking of building apartments here," he said. "Maybe condominiums. There's plenty of land."

Her fingers stilled on the doorknob.

His voice, *that* voice, sounded heartbreakingly familiar.

She put a hand to her throat. No. It couldn't be.

"Do you want to check out the upstairs?" Candee asked.

"There's only one bathroom, right?"

"Right, and there's admittedly a lack of closet space," Candee said. "Naturally, all these updates are possible, though a character-laden house like this is special."

He chuckled. "Character-laden? I like that."

"We Realtors try our best, Lincoln."

Lincoln Reid. Here? In Roses?

She closed her eyes. Lincoln's voice, the voice of the guy she'd once dated, once been head-over-heels in love with, whispered through her mind.

She often intended to bring closure to her past. But not here. Not today. She needed more than a minute to prepare.

"No matter what, Shay, we'll tackle life together," he'd once declared. Everyone else called her by her legal name. Not him. He'd given her the nickname Shay—*his* nickname for her. "We'll give each other courage to fight any obstacles and come out together on the other side."

They'd come out on the other side, all right. Though not together.

End of Excerpt *1-800-NEW YEAR* by Josie Riviera ***

Want more? Keep reading *1-800-NEW YEAR*

FREE on Kindle Unlimited!

ABOUT THE AUTHOR

Josie Riviera is a *USA TODAY* bestselling author of contemporary, inspirational, and historical sweet romances that read like Hallmark movies. She lives in the Charlotte, NC, area with her wonderfully supportive husband. They share their home with an adorable shih tzu, who constantly needs grooming, and live in an old house forever needing renovations.

Become a member of my Read and Review VIP Facebook group for exclusive giveaways and ARCs.

To connect with Josie, visit her webpage and subscribe to her newsletter. As a thank-you, she'll send you a free sweet romance novella directly to your inbox.

josieriviera.com

X Ⓞ ⓐ BB f g Ⓟ ▶ in 🅟 d

IND'TALE MAGAZINE REVIEW
AND 5 STAR READER REVIEWS

CONTEMPORARY ROMANCE:

"Belle Boots loves horses. So much so that she has made them her life's work by running an equine therapy practice. Looking for a change in scenery, she takes on a fixer-upper and goes against the norm of her nomadic ways in exchange for something more stable.

She returns to her childhood home, Wilmington, and it's there she meets Andrew Bransfield. Unfortunately, it doesn't seem as though she can stay. Determined to keep Belle in town to help his daughter, Andrew sets out to build her the perfect barn for her horses. In doing so, he may just end up building something more.

Ms. Riviera has created a beautiful, moving sweet romance that will resonate with readers long after the book ends! Belle is a heroine that can be admired and loved right off the bat. Her passion for her patients and her drive for adventure give her a beautiful heart mixed with a fun energy. Andrew is a driven man who has a fear of animals. He is strong and steady, and when the two of them get together, their chemistry is natural and believable. This book is part of a series, but it stands alone nicely. There are a few moments when the conflict doesn't feel quite believable, but overall the book is smooth and a joy to read that will fill many with hope. This is a great book for lovers of sweet romance and small town settings!"

5 Star Reader Reviews:

"I loved this cute summer read. From the banter between Andrew and Belle, to their honesty and struggles. And lets not forget the fainting goats!! A few twists and turns along the way. Will confident Andrew learn to prioritize his life and forgive past hurts? Can Belle give in to this tender-hearted and romantic man without compromising? A clean swoon-worthy tale I highly recommend!" - Amazon Reviewer

PRAISE AND AWARDS

USA TODAY bestselling author

#21 Amazon Bestseller Contemporary Western Fiction

#37 Amazon Bestseller Scottish Historical Romance

#21 Amazon Bestseller Contemporary Western Fiction

ALSO BY JOSIE RIVIERA

Seeking Patience

Seeking Catherine (always Free!)

Seeking Fortune

Seeking Charity

Seeking Rachel

The Seeking Series

Oh Danny Boy

I Love You More

A Snowy White Christmas

A Portuguese Christmas

Holiday Hearts Book Bundle Volume One

Holiday Hearts Book Bundle Volume Two

Holiday Hearts Book Bundle Volume Three

Holiday Hearts Book Bundle Volume Four

Holiday Hearts Book Bundle Volume Five

Candleglow and Mistletoe

Maeve (Perfect Match)

A Love Song To Cherish

A Christmas To Cherish

A Valentine To Cherish

A Christmas Puppy To Cherish

A Homecoming To Cherish

A Summer To Cherish

Romance Stories To Cherish

Romance Stories To Cherish Volume Two

Cherished Hearts Six Book Volume

Aloha To Love

Sweet Peppermint Kisses

Valentine Hearts Boxed Set

1-800-CUPID

1-800-CHRISTMAS

1-800-IRELAND

1-800-SUMMER

1-800-NEW YEAR

The 1-800-Series Sweet Contemporary Romance Bundle

Irish Hearts Sweet Romance Bundle

Holly's Gift

A Chocolate-Box Christmas

A Chocolate-Box New Years

A Chocolate-Box Valentine

A Chocolate-Box Summer Breeze

A Chocolate-Box Christmas Wish

A Chocolate-Box Irish Wedding

Chocolate-Box Hearts

Chocolate-Box Hearts Volume Two

Chocolate-Box Double Hearts

Recipes From The Heart

Leading Hearts

New Year Hearts

SENIOR HEARTS

Summer Hearts

Christmas in the Air (1-800-Book)

A Very Christian Christmas

The 1-800-Series Volume Two

The 1-800-Series Complete

Christmas Tails of the Heart

Cocoa's Christmas Love

Pawfect Christmas Hearts

Pink Coral Island

Whispers of Love in Sweetwater Springs

Whispers of Maple Memories in Sweetwater Springs

Whispers of Holiday Magic in Sweetwater Springs

Whispers of Sweetwater Springs

A Harvest of Miracles

A Winter Promise

A Season Out of Time

Hearts and Horseshoes

1-800-CUPIDON (French Edition)

1-800-CUPDO (Spanish Edition)

1-800-AMOR (German Edition)

Most books are available in ebook, audiobook, paperback, Large Print paperback and Hardcover.

Many are FREE on Kindle Unlimited!

A GIFT FOR YOU

To keep up on newly released ebooks, paperbacks, Large Print Paperbacks, audiobooks, as well as exclusive sales, sign up for Josie's Newsletter today.

As a thank you, I'll send you a Free PDF: The Beauty Of

Josie's Newsletter

Did you know that according to a Yale University study, people who read books live longer?